NEVER TOO LATE

NEVER TOO LATE

Elizabeth Tettmar

This title first published in Great Britain 1996 by
SEVERN HOUSE PUBLISHERS LTD of
9–15 High Street, Sutton, Surrey SM1 1DF.
Originally published 1983 under the title *Kitty
Tredennick* and pseudonym *Elizabeth Spence*.
First published in the USA 1996 by
SEVERN HOUSE PUBLISHERS INC. of
595 Madison Avenue, New York, NY 10022.

British Library Cataloguing in Publication Data

Tettmar, Elizabeth
  Never too late
  1. English fiction – 20th century
  I. Title
  823.9'14 [F]

ISBN 0-7278-5190-X

For Norah (Nornie).

Typeset by Palimpsest Book Production Limited,
Polmont, Stirlingshire, Scotland.
Printed and bound in Great Britain by
Hartnolls Ltd, Bodmin, Cornwall.

ONE

There was a bright moon the night that the *Bolivier* sailed out of Falmouth harbour with Harvey Stephens on board. Kitty stood on the broad walk beneath Pendennis Castle watching the tall ship sailing away. There was just sufficient wind to fill the top sails, sufficient to blow the ship out of Carrick Roads and towards the sea.

She waved but it was an empty gesture. Even if Harvey were on deck he would be unable to see her. She was but a pin-point of shadow hidden by the deeper shadow of the castle wall rearing behind her. Across the bay a similar castle stood watchful over the harbour of St. Mawes.

Compared with Falmouth, St. Mawes was of little importance then. But it had the advantage of facing south and the sun attracted visitors. Now, with its cottages whitened by moonlight it held an illusion of beauty—an illusion, because behind many a cottage-door poverty and want were continuous battles.

It was only the day before that Harvey had sailed Kitty across to St. Mawes in one of her father's boats. They had left it at the quayside and then walked over the moors to the deserted village of Tregorra.

Fifty years before, in 1837, Tregorra had been a thriving little fishing community, but now all that remained was a derelict church and the foundations of cottages. Everything else had been swept away in a gale which had hammered the village for three days and nights. The sea which had sustained the community for many generations had turned into a destroying monster swallowing up that which it had helped to build. Now wild fuchsia and sea-thrift softened the scars, and jackdaws nested on the stone ledges of the church tower. It was an isolated place—far out on a tongue of land. Few people cared to walk so far and it was too treacherous to reach by sea.

But to Kitty and Harvey that mild spring day it was the very solace they needed. They wanted this short time to be utterly alone. They didn't know when they would meet again.

Kitty was slight, only reaching as far as Harvey's shoulder. "My little Celtic Princess", he teased her. She was a true Celtic beauty. Her black hair rippled to her waist, her dark eyes tilted slightly upwards beneath finely arched brows. A 'Gypsy changeling' her father had once dubbed her, for nobody else in the family was so dark. Maggie, Kitty's elder sister by six years, took after her mother, her features already set in a placid expression, her figure beginning to thicken.

Kitty had fallen in love with Harvey with all the depths of her wilful passionate heart. He had come to work for her father when she was just fourteen—he was ten years older—tall, fair with deepset grey eyes. Though Cornish born he favoured a Scottish grandmother in his colouring.

He came from a wealthy family. Kitty, trudging up the long hill to school, could remember the Stephens' residence set amid green lawns and with terraces that commanded a view beyond the harbour to the open sea, and where it was said, Old Man Stephens sat with his telescope watching his ships like great white birds homing in to land.

But time was running out for the tall ships which in their hey-day had crowded the harbour with a forest of masts. Steam was rapidly replacing sail and ever since 1852 when the last Post Office packet sailed out of the harbour, Falmouth as a prosperous port had declined. Southampton had now usurped the important position which Falmouth had held for so long.

Sailing ships bringing passengers from the Americas or clippers bringing tea and spice from the Far East had made for Falmouth as the first port of call. Now steamships, cutting the passage time by half, could bypass Falmouth and make straight for Southampton nearly two hundred miles nearer to the commercial centres of London and Bristol.

Old Mr Stephens ignored the warning signals. He scoffed at the idea that steam would ever replace sail. He scoffed too at the idea of Falmouth becoming a forgotten port. He had the reputation of being a man of sound business sense and integrity. His patronage helped many a small ships'-chandler like Kitty's father, to make a good living. Kitty remembered as a small child her father rowing her out to meet one of the Stephens' ships when it put down anchor, her lap full of violets and primroses she had picked in the lanes. The crew would accept her offerings with gratitude. They were the first growing things they had seen for six months.

The City Fathers could see the writing on the wall, and

were already discussing means of propping up Falmouth's economy by turning it into a sea-side resort—perhaps one to rival the fashiionable resorts on the south and east coasts. But for the time being they kept such radical ideas to themselves. The Cornish people still liked to think of themselves as a race apart and viewed visitors with suspicion.

And all the time the half-empty ships of the Stephens' line were losing money and when Old Man Stephens died the only legacy he left was a massive debt. Already ailing, Mrs Stephens went off to spend the few months still remaining to her with her sister at Truro.

To Harvey, still at college, fell the task of selling the home and auctioning the furniture, horses and carriages. Even the last of the ships had to go. It took him nearly three years to get his father's affairs straightened out, then he came to Mr Tredennick to ask for work—any work. He had always liked and respected Joseph Tredennick.

But Tredennick, like the other ships'-chandlers was going through a rough patch himself. For the time being he was managing to make out by doing a little boat building on the side. Nothing too ambitious—he hadn't the capital for that, but there was a demand for small boats for sale and for hire.

Harvey showed a flair for boat design, he had been studying as a marine architect, and Jospeh Tredennick soon realized that with money and influence he could have gone far. As it was he could not afford to pay Harvey any more than he paid the other men in the yard, and if Harvey felt any bitterness at his changed circumstances, he did not show it.

Sloe-eyed Kitty could not keep away from the boat-yard. She skipped in and out of the tackle shops, climbed the sail lofts, hopped around the anchor forges inhaling with delight the tang of pitch and wood shavings. She loved the very sight and smell of the sea and rued the day she had been born a girl which prevented any dreams of becoming a seaman—that is until she first became aware of Harvey standing motionless in his overalls and gazing over the harbour with such longing in his eyes that her heart leapt. From that moment she was all woman.

Harvey had turned and caught her staring at him and had smiled and called her 'Kitten'. To him she was still a child—the Guv'ner's pretty, younger daughter.

It was when she was about seventeen that the ready smile he always had for her took a subtle change, and the grey eyes instead of watching the sea would follow her lithe movements about the boatyard. The change in his attitude did not go unobserved, and Joseph scowled. One night at supper he said; "I don't want you hanging about the yard anymore. Is that understood, Miss?"

Kitty pouted but knew better than to disobey her father. From then on she stayed at home and helped more in the house. To everyone's surprise Maggie had got a job as a milliner. The pocket-money her father allowed her wasn't enough, she said, to buy all the clothes she now needed.

Now needed—Kitty pricked up her ears. Maggie had never shown much interest in clothes before. Had she got a sweetheart? Could it be Dave Williams, a giant of a man with hardly a word to say for himself who worked on the pilchard boats and made sheep's eyes at Maggie in chapel on Sundays?

Then one afternoon on an errand for her mother in Killigrew Street, Kitty's sharp eyes had seen her sister being escorted across the road by a foreigner from London. She recognized him as the man who often came to the yard to hire one of the rowing-boats. At first sight she had taken an instinctive dislike to him and had recoiled from the look in his pale, protruding eyes. He was on holiday and staying at an inn near the harbour.

When he wasn't out fishing he hired a bicycle and explored the surrounding countryside.

He came at Easter and again in August and then late October. He was always smartly dressed and very courteous and saw more and more of Maggie. Kitty realized that her parents were encouraging the courtship, and now Maggie cut her front hair and frizzed it into a fringe and preened in front of the mirror. Poor Dave still came regularly to chapel but went away without speaking after the service.

"You're not treating Dave right," stormed Kitty one Sunday evening. "You've been friends ever since school-days, now you hardly bother to notice him. And why are you all dressed up? Where are you going? To see old Cow's Eyes, I shouldn't wonder."

Colour mounted in Maggie's cheeks. "You needn't be so vulgar. Mr Beatty can't help his eyes. You don't know him—he's a perfect gentleman."

"Oh, and who told you? What do you know about him except for his name—Adrian—and that he's about thirty and comes from London and spends holidays down here?"

"It stands to reason he must have money or he couldn't afford so many holidays. And I can tell he's a gentleman by his manners," and Maggie buttoned on her gloves with a self-satisfied smirk.

Kitty's eyes snapped angrily. "Maggie Tredennick, I can tell by your voice you don't care a scrap for him at all. You're just after his money. I'd be ashamed if I were you."

"Oh you would, would you!" The shaft had gone home and Maggie turned on her sister in fury. "Then let me tell you, you won't find it so funny when you reach my age and no chance of a good marriage. You know the position we're in now—Father is only just scraping a living. We used to have a little general to do the housework; now you

10

and I do it all between us and Mother does the cooking. It's economise—economise—all the time. D'you know what I overheard Mother and Father discussing the other evening? Giving up this big old house and renting a cottage down near the harbour! How would you like that?"

Kitty's heart leapt. There was nothing she would have liked better. She had no pretensions about big houses. She would love to live within sound of the sea—to be awakened by the screech of gulls in the morning. But Maggie had one final thrust.

"And why do you think Father has stopped you going to the boatyard? Because he's seen the way you make up to Harvey, that's what. You don't think you stand a chance there, do you? Harvey might pass the time of day flirting with you, but when it comes to marriage he'll want a wife with money and influence. Someone who could help set him up in business again. You'll just be wasting your time there, you'll see."

Kitty had been unable to find the right retort at the time, but when Maggie had gone she had thrown herself on the bed and given way to a storm of tears. When she had calmed down, and her storms never lasted long, she meditated some time over her sister's words. Then she filled the bowl on the washstand with water and splashed her reddened eyes. There was only one way to find out what Harvey felt about her and that was to ask. It was as simple as that.

Maggie had worn a straw hat with a stiff bow at the front that had been starched until it was as hard as a board. Kitty disdained hats when she could and now draped a tulle scarf about her hair, well aware that the soft pink colour enhanced the glow in her cheeks.

She crept noiselessly downstairs. Her mother and father were sitting in the parlour, talking, and she could hear their voices plainly. Her father was saying;

"He seems a worthy enough chap, and always very respectful towards me, I must say. I believe he means well by our Maggie. I just wish we knew more about his background, that's all."

And her mother's answer, barely audible above the clicking of her knitting needles; "If he does ask Maggie to marry him it will be a wonderful opportunity for her, there's nothing here now in Falmouth for the young folk. But it's Kitty I'm worried about. I know she's head over heels in love with Harvey Stephens, and she's such a child still in many ways. I don't want to see her hurt."

Kitty held her breath as she awaited her father's answer. It had come slowly and ponderously, after much thought.

"Harvey Stephens is an honourable man, but he's not in a position yet to support a wife, and will have to go much further afield to make a good living, and I've told him so many a time. He knows my views on Kitty too. He won't ask for her hand until he has something substantial to back him up."

Kitty had crept away feeling like some small bruised creature seeking comfort. All this talk about a good living and to be able to support a wife—what had that to do with love? She didn't want money or position or fine clothes; she just wanted Harvey and she was going to find him and tell him so right now, because she knew her father was right in one thing. Harvey was too honourable to make the first move.

But when she reached the narrow crowded street off the harbour near his lodgings, rollicking seamen—many the worse for drink—called after her and ogled her boldly and her courage began to waver. If she called for Harvey the word could get back to her father, and though normally a mild man he could, when his wrath was aroused, be formidable. She began to regret her mad impulse especially when she saw her path was blocked by a knot of Breton sailors, their arms entwined about one another's necks, all singing lustily. How could she push her way past them?

There was a touch on her arm, and turning she encountered Adrian Beatty. Instinctively she shrank away.

"Why, Miss Kitty!"—in his suavest manner. "What are you doing in this unsalubrious part of Falmouth?"

Kitty didn't know what unsalubrious meant. The expression on his face made her feel uneasy. Even after days of sea air he had not lost his unhealthy pallor. She found herself lying glibly—too glibly. "I'm looking for Maggie. She's wanted at home."

He raised his brows and smiled slightly. "Now isn't that fortunate. I'm due to meet your sister by the Town Hall. Perhaps you will allow me to escort you."

His grip tightened on her arm. The Breton sailors would have been preferable to his unwelcome attention. Her relief was obvious when she saw Harvey approaching. Adrian also saw him and his arm dropped. The two men barely acknowledged one another and Kitty sensed a mutual antipathy. When Adrain was out of earshot Harvey said; "What on earth are you doing here?"—and his tone was brusque,

Tears sprang into her eyes. "Don't scold, Harvey, I had to see you," and in that narrow street with the foreign sailors milling about them, Kitty opened her heart to the man she loved. With unusual gentleness, Harvey led her to the privacy of a courtyard.

"Kitty—Kitty—you are still such a child. Of course I'm not searching for a rich wife—what have I to offer any wife, let alone a rich one?" He tilted her chin and looked earnestly at her tear-stained face. Kitty realized then how ill-judged Maggie's words had been.

Harvey loved her. It was there plain to see in the expression in his eyes. He couldn't disguise the fact any

13

more than she could hide her feelings for him.

There was more than love in Harvey's expression, there was a longing too that sent her pulse racing. He lowered his voice; "Oh pet, you're still so young—other, better chances for you might come along. You're as pretty as a peach—many suitors will beat a path to your door and I don't mean to stand in their way."

"But Harvey, there'll never be anyone else for me but you—,"

"Listen darling, I may be poor but I have my pride. When I come to claim you for my wife I won't come empty-handed, I'm adamant on that. Until then we must both have patience."

"Are we engaged then?" she had asked with such hope in her voice that he had laughed, swung her off her feet in a bear's hug and kissed her with such ardour she had been left breathless. It was her first kiss and she had hoped for a repeat, but instead Harvey had cupped her face in his hands and said;

"Yes, my little precious, I think we can say we are engaged. But we must keep it secret otherwise your father may send me packing."

That has been six months ago. Kitty had tried to be patient but it had not come easily to her. On the few occasions when she and Harvey had managed a secret meeting she had found him strangely withdrawn. He said he had a plan but wouldn't discuss it with her until it was fully executed as he didn't want to raise her hopes. When he did in fact reveal what he had in mind, far from raising her hopes, she was pitched into the depths of despair.

He had been in touch with an old college friend who had emigrated to America and made good out there. Oliver Sutcliffe had written of the vast new steel-works being erected in Pennsylvania, and steel was the raw material for the steamships now being built in their thousands.

14

"Don't you see, Kitty, the opportunities that opens up? There might be a chance for me in one of the big ship-building offices as a designer. Oliver's got on—he'll put in a word for me. Once I'm established I'll send for you and we'll make a new life in a new country together."

Kitty could find no words to counteract his but her heart was heavy. How long would it be—months—years—before she could join him? There was no answer.

Naturally enough her father was as enthusiastic about the idea as Harvey himself, saying that if he were young again it was what he would do. America was the land of opportunity—the country for the young in heart. In a more practical fashion he obtained for Harvey a free passage on the old trading-ship *Bolivier*, which was sailing for Southampton with a load of china clay. It would save Harvey the railway fare, and from Southampton he could book passage to New York in the steam packet *Eugenie*.

Her mother and father were not insensitive to Kitty's suffering. It was they who suggested that she and Harvey should spend his last day in England alone and together. Mr Tredennick loaned them a sailing dinghy and Mrs Tredennick packed a picnic basket. Even Maggie, who was a kind girl at heart, lent Kitty her lace-edged parasol.

But Kitty didn't worry about her complexion. The sun had already darkened it to the colour of gold, and Maggie's parasol lay furled under one of the thwarts.

They had eaten their lunch amid the ruins of Tregorra. From where they sat on the broken step of the church porch, they could see the *Bolivier* tied up in Falmouth harbour. "There she is," Harvey pointed her out. "She sails in less than twelve hours."

"Don't—don't." Kitty had cried out in anguish. "I can't bear to think of it. Don't spoil this lovely time together."

His arm held her more closely. "Then you mustn't

spoil it, either. Remember, you promised no tears today. My last memory of you must be a happy one."

It was easy enough to smile when he looked at her like that, but inside she went on grieving for all the empty days and months they would be parted. On an impulse she sprang to her feet—anything would be better than sitting, just sitting, while the precious minutes ticked away. "Let's go into the church. Let's see what's left of it."

The stained glass windows had gone, but the sun shone through the apertures giving the light a strangely haunting quality. "It still seems like a church—it still feels holy," said Kitty in a hushed voice.

Harvey had gone up to the sanctuary. The altar had been swept away with the other church furnishings, but on a stone shelf above a pair of swallows were building a nest, and their twittering brought a semblance of life back to the deserted church. Kitty joined Harvey and slipped her thin brown hand into his. "We could be married here," she said. "I mean it's still a church—it's still consecrated. We could marry each other in the sight of God."

He looked away as if not trusting himself to reveal the desire in his heart. "Is that what you want, my pet?"

"Yes, oh Harvey, yes. It will help me when you are gone. I'll feel that I really belong to you."

Hand in hand they stood before the altar place. What they could remember of the marriage service they said aloud, in turn. The sun was their attendant, the swallows their witnesses and the sea murmuring in the distance, the choir.

"I, Harvey, take thee Catherine to be my lawful wedded wife, to love and to cherish—,"

"I, Catherine, take thee Harvey, to be my lawful wedded husband—,"

Their voices faded, even the swallows were silenced, wary of their presence. Harvey slipped off the signet ring he always wore on his little finger. "It was my mother's," he said, as he placed it on Kitty's third finger. She bent her head and kissed it, then raised her lips eagerly to his.

"We are married now, aren't we, Harvey? We are really married in the sight of God?"

What doubts he had he kept to himself. This warm, passionate girl was offering herself to him. His love was just as strong, and even more difficult to control. Kitty's arms went round his neck, her lips parted on a tiny sigh. "Take me Harvey—carry me out to the cliff top. Love me, my own dearest husband."

TWO

Now it was two a.m. Seagulls roosting on the buoys at the harbour mouth mewed restlessly. To Kitty it seemed as if they were crying for her. She could no longer see the *Bolivier*, its tall mast had disappeared behind St. Anthony's Head. She shivered and drew her shawl closer about her narrow shoulders.

Never had she felt so utterly alone as she turned her back on the castle and began the steep walk back to the sleeping town. The moon cast shadows and every tree seemed a menace and the rustle of their leaves sounded like ominous whispers.

But grief overcame her fear of the night. "Harvey—oh Harvey," she moaned brokenly. He had gone off so jauntily—her fair-headed handsome husband—so confident of the future, leaving her with nagging doubts. For her the future seemed blank and uncertain.

Blinded by tears, not heeding where she was treading, she tripped over a kerb and would have fallen but for a helping hand. For one incredulous second she wondered if Harvey had not left after all, then a figure moved into the moonlight and she recognized Adrian Beatty.

She pulled her arm away and walked on, but he only quickened his step to keep pace with her. "Do your parents know you are out at this hour," he asked blandly.

"I don't see that's any concern of yours."

They walked in silence. It didn't even cross her mind to wonder why he was abroad at such a time oo. She soon forgot about him, indulging in a bitter-sweet longing for Harvey, and remembering with kindled cheeks the delights of their last hours together. She stopped at the tradesmen's entrance to her house. A prowling cat brushed against her ankles. As she put her hand on the gate Adrain spoke again. "Goodnight, or should I say *good morning,*" Miss Kitty?"

She thanked him prettily for escorting her so gallantly through the dark, loading her voice with irony which was not lost on him. Catching her unawares he swung her round and drew her to him, fastening his full wet lips on hers. Her stifled cries were lost under the pressure of his mouth.

"Don't struggle, my little dear," he muttered. "I've waited long enough for this. Haven't you realized I've only been dancing attendance on your sister just on the opportunity of seeing you. Now that that stiff-necked admirer of yours is out of the way, you might give a thought to ne. I'm a far better match."

She pulled herself away and struck him full in the face. He laughed silently, his teeth barely showing, then kissed her again, forcing her mouth open.

She was on the point of screaming, risking her father's reaction to her nighttime leave-taking when like the cat—

another night prowler—and just as quietly, he disappeared into the shadow of the trees and was gone.

She was still shaking when she crept into bed beside the sleeping Maggie. How dare he treat her like one of those hussies who hung about the dockside for foreign seaman? She had scrubbed her mouth with her face flannel until it stung—but could still sense the touch of his wet lips. Maggie moved in her sleep and gave a little sigh. No doubt dreaming of her so eminently respectable suitor. She, Kitty, would soon enlighten her about that, then realized that she couldn't. How could she hurt Maggie who for the past year had believed herself to be courted by a very eligible man. The fraud—the odious hypocrite. She was angrier on Maggie's part than on her own. It was of Harvey she was thinking when she finally cried herself to sleep.

It took three weeks before the aching longing for Harvey began to wear off. Three weeks before she could think of him without eyes welling or speak of him without breaking down. Her mother, sensible woman that she was, saw that Kitty was kept so busy she had little time for fretting. Maggie, even more practical, suggested she started on her bottom drawer, it would be something to occupy the lonely hours. A labour of love that turned out to be for Kitty, unlike Maggie, was no needlewoman, but now she sat most afternoons stitching cambric camisoles and petticoats; embroidering corset covers and making winter and summer nightgowns, and into every stitch went a thought for Harvey.

Adrian had returned to London; on business, Maggie informed her family. Nobody knew what Adrian's business was—he was reticent about his private life but they all assumed it was a lucrative one for he had the appearance of a man of means. Kitty was delighted to have him four hundred miles away and with no likelihood of coming upon him suddenly when out shopping.

Dave Williams reappeared, escorting Maggie home from the chapel on Sunday evenings, but she did nothing to encourage him and did not invite him in for a late cup of tea as in the old days. Kitty liked and respected Dave. He was a large, shambling man with a limited vocabulary, but he had whittled her first toy out of a piece of drift-wood, and she was disappointed that Maggie couldn't see, in spite of his humble circumstances, he was a better man than Adrian Beatty.

Day after day she watched for the post, hoping and praying for a letter from Harvey. The chances were small as the time gap between disembarking from the *Bolivier* and catching the steam-packet from Southampton would leave him little time for writing letters. Her hopes were pinned on the thought that he might have sent her a verbal message with one of the crew of the *Bolivier*. But it would be several weeks before it was due back in Falmouth.

More than a month went by. Now something new began to gnaw at the core of her unhappiness, fretting her with a fresh worry. It couldn't be possible—it *mustn't* be possible. It was a possibility she couldn't face.

One lunch time her father came in looking unusually grave. Maggie stayed at the shop so only Kitty and her mother awaited him in the morning-room. For the first time Kitty noticed how deep the grooves were that ran from his nose down to each corner of his mouth, as if the flesh had been eaten away by anxious thoughts. Today he looked more tired than usual. He called her mother into the kitchen and spoke to her in low tones. Kitty heard a stifled cry, then her father's voice again; "You stay here—I'll tell the lass."

Tell the lass—herself? Her heart began to thump. She fought an impulse to lock the door—to keep her father out. But she stayed at the table and watched him with fearful eyes as he took a chair opposite. "The *Bolivier* is back," he said.

She jumped up with a glad cry. It was good news—not bad. What a fool she had been to jump to conclusions. "I must go—I must see if there is any message from Harvey," she cried. Her father pulled her back.

"Child, I want you to be brave. I have bad news—the worst—,"

"Harvey?" Her hand flew to her mouth.

"Not only Harvey—. Every man, woman, and child on that ill-fated ship. It developed engine-trouble and blew up off the Azores. The one survivor died later from his wounds."

She stared at him with uncomprehending eyes. "How do you know all this?"

"A French barque witnessed the accident and picked up the survivor. It was becalmed for days before it could continue its journey, then it went on to Le Havre. Goodness knows why the news has taken so long to get back here. The skipper of the *Bolivier* got it from another French seaman. Come Kitty, sit down—"

A scream began in Kitty's throat and tore its way through her trembling lips, but no sound came—only a moan as she slipped senseless onto the floor.

When she came round she was in her own bed and her mother and Maggie were bending over her. Her mother's eyes were red-rimmed and Maggie's full of compassion. But she didn't want their grief or their compassion—she just wanted Harvey, and she began to scream his name aloud until suddenly Maggie grasped her by her shoulders and began to shake her.

"Stop it—stop screaming like that—it won't bring Harvey back, and it won't do you any good either. You've always loved the sea—always wanted to go to sea yourself—now what has it done to you!"

"Harvey—Harvey—" Kitty whimpered, heedless of Maggie's words. Her mother pushed Maggie away. "It's too soon for that sort of talk," she said. "Can't you see the poor child's in shock. Go and fetch your father's brandy."

They had to force the burning liquid down Kitty's throat. She gasped and spluttered, sobbed a little, then lay limp in her mother's arms. "My husband—my precious husband—" she moaned.

"What can she mean—'husband'?" Maggie queried.

" 'Tis but the shock, she'll sleep now—the brandy will see to that. Stay with her, Maggie. I'll go down to your father. The news is not good for him, either." They had kept from the girls that capital they could ill afford had been invested in the *Eugenie*.

Kitty soon discovered that life had to go on. Hearts might be breaking, but beds had to be made, dishes washed and meals prepared. In a dull sort of way she wondered why the news hadn't reached them sooner. Certainly, no newspapers were delivered to their house any more; that was one of her mother's small economies, but somebody must have known—could have informed them. Anyway, what did it matter? The whys and wherefores were now unimportant. All she could think about was her golden-haired Harvey wantonly killed with all his life before him. By day she learned to keep her grief under control. Only at night, lying beside the sleeping Maggie, did she indulge in tears, until even tears ceased to give relief and were replaced instead by a constant ache.

Red, white and blue flags were going up in the streets of Falmouth. Red, white and blue flowers appeared in window-boxes and gardens. Red, white and blue bunting streamed from the masts of the ships in harbour. It was 1887 and every town, village and hamlet in the land was celebrating Queen Victoria's Golden Jubilee. There were going to be balls and banquets and firework displays to mark the occasion and bonfires all over Cornwall.

Adrian Beatty reappeared in a natty grey suit with a

matching felt hat. He wore a blue cravat with his high starched collar, and there was always a red rose in his button-hole. He now sported a gold-topped cane and hired a dog-cart, and called on Maggie and took her driving in the long summer evenings.

If he had heard of the fate of the *Eugenie* he made no mention of it in Kitty's presence. When he called for Maggie Kitty always slipped out of the room, but was aware that his colourless eyes followed her every movement. One day her father announced, somewhat smugly, that Alderman Scammell had given him four complimentary tickets to the ball the City Fathers were holding at the castle.

"Why should he have done that, Joseph?" asked his wife with surprise. The Tredennicks neither entertained nor were asked out socially since the fall in their fortune.

"Perhaps because he still owes me for the punt I made for young Royal Scammell's twenty-first birthday. No, I won't be uncharitable, perhaps the good man thinks we all deserve a treat. Anyway, it's a grand chance to put on our best bibs and tuckers and go out and enjoy ourselves for once," with a sideways look at Kitty.

"Then you must excuse me, dear, my dancing days are over," and it was certainly true that Mrs Tredennick tired very quickly these days. Kitty would have preferred to stay home with her mother, but neither Maggie nor her father would hear of it.

Kitty felt too listless to care whether she went to the ball or not, but when her mother urged her to she agreed. She had more than grief on her mind these days and one night of revelry might help her forget the sickening dread that she was carrying Harvey's child. She tried not to think of the effect this news would have on her family. She herself still believed with childlike faith that she was really married to Harvey in the eyes of God, but she was also adult enough to know that the spiritual side apart, a certain legal paper was necessary to save her from disgrace. If she only had herself to think about she would have borne Harvey's child gladly, but there were her parents and she knew well enough what a scandal would do to them.

Maggie went to work at once making herself a white muslin gown for the ball. "And what are you planning to wear?" she asked Kitty one evening as with keen delight she stitched the last of the frilling about the neck and sleeves. "Your green silk? It's old and a bit on the short side but it's a lovely colour and suits you so well."

"I wondered whether I could borrow your black lawn," said Kitty quietly.

"My old black lawn! Oh Kitty, you can't wear mourning for the rest of your life—you're still so young. You used to be so gay. Always skipping about—always singing—you're so quiet now, somehow so spiritless. No, I won't let you borrow my dress, it's only encouraging you to be morbid."

Kitty could not admit that her own black dress, which she had worn daily since the news of Harvey's death, was already too tight round the waist for her though she had let out some of the tucks. The present fashion of gowns drawn tightly across the abdomen and drawn into a bustle at the back did nothing to disguise a thickening figure. She could almost wish that the crinolines of her mother's day would come back. She had often heard her mother remark that a woman could hide her pregnancy up to the seventh month when she had been young.

Maggie relented as she always did. "Oh, all right then, I'll lend you my lawn, but it will be miles too big for you."

"I'll have time to alter it."

On the night of the ball they went to their mother's room to show themselves off. She was lying fully-clothed on the bed, but sat up as they entered. What a contrast they made in their black and white gowns. She couldn't help thinking that Maggie looked like an overblown rose in hers. It was too girlish for her, and had too much trimming, but excitement had lent something attractive to Maggie's full face and her eyes which were her best feature were alight with expectation because she had learnt that Adrian Beatty had also obtained a ticket for the ball. But when Mrs Tredennick looked at Kitty her heart fell. The black dress drained all colour from the child's face and her head seemed bowed with the weight of her hair which Maggie had braided and coiled in the latest fashion. Still, there was a look of quiet dignity about her, and the cream lace at her wrists and throat offset the plainness of the dress. Mrs Tredennick was pleased to see that Kitty was wearing the cameo brooch her grandmother had left her. Perhaps she could be persuaded to take an interest in her appearance again.

Their father came along to hurry them up. "Come along, that's enough prinking and preening, what makes you girls think anyone will have eyes for you? With the officers in their dress uniforms, you women won't get a look in," and he winked at his wife.

In spite of herself Kitty found her spirits rising when they entered the main hall of the castle. Flags and bunting draped the stone walls and there were enough potted plants about to make it look like an orangery. Fires large enough to roast oxen blazed in the two fireplaces, and were needed even in summer for the outside warmth couldn't penetrate the solid walls. Their father was right. No matter how colourful and stylish the ladies' gowns they were easily outshone by the brillancy of the officers—like tropical birds in their reds and blues emblazoned with gold lace and braid.

Under his breath their father said they reminded him of strutting young cockerels showing off their fine feathers, but the girls knew he was just as proud of the garrison as they were. He was feeling stiff and ill-at-ease in his own finery—the suit he wore to his wedding and stored in moth-balls ever since—and this was making him testy.

In her black gown, sitting on a gilt chair close to a pillar Kitty was overlooked by eager young men out for fresh partners. Maggie romped happily through gavottes and polkas, her face as red as a peony. Kitty was sipping a glass of fruit cup when a familiar voice at her elbow said; "May I have the pleasure of this waltz, Miss Kitty?"

She felt the colour rise in her cheeks and fade again. She turned with an angry retort, then as she looked up at Adrian and saw the overt desire in his eyes a sudden flash of insight showed a way out of her predicament.

As distasteful as it seemed, as much as she shrank from the idea, it would prevent the scandal which would break her mother's heart and deepen the grooves of worry on her father's face.

Adrain wanted her. Very well then—he should have her—but only as his wife. She raised her eyes again forcing her lips into a rigid smile, then offered him her hand.

"It will be a pleasure Mr Beatty," she said, and allowed herself to be waltzed away in his arms.

THREE

When Kitty announced a week later at the supper table that she had accepted Adrian Beatty's proposal of marriage, she was met by a silence so suffocating that it sounded like the surge of sea pounding in her ears. Then Maggie, white to the lips, rose abruptly and left the room. They heard the slam of an upstairs door.

Joseph Tredennick put down his cup of tea. "Did I hear aright? That fellow asked *you* to marry him?"

"And I said I would."

"Don't be pert with me, miss."

"I didn't intend to be pert. Please, Father—"

But Joseph was too enraged to listen to excuses. He banged his fist on the table. "What's his game, I'd like to know. Chasing after Maggie for the best part of a year, then suddenly transferring his attentions to you. It's a hugger-mugger kind of a goings-on if you ask me. And what about you, miss—what kind of an underhanded game have you been playing? Making up to your sister's sweetheart when all the time we thought your heart was breaking over Harvey."

Kitty hung her head. The very mention of Harvey's name had brought a rush of tears to her eyes.

Mrs Tredennick put a restraining hand on her husband's arm. "Hush Joe, it doesn't help to carry on so. Kitty hasn't done anything wrong. If you haven't noticed how the wind's been blowing this past month then you are more of an old stump than I thought."

His wife was the only one who could calm Joseph when he lost his temper, but this time he was determined not to be placated too easily. "What d'you mean how the wind's been blowing? Talk sense, woman!"

The shocked Kitty looked up. She had never heard her father use that tone to her mother before. But her mother only smiled her customary smile and gave her husband's arm a playful pat.

"Why, 'tis been that plain to see that Kitty's been the attraction. I'm sorry for Maggie, and I don't like it anymore than you do the way Adrian has been playing one of our girls against the other, but Maggie has partly herself to blame. She practically threw herself at him in the first place. She'll not suffer from a broken heart—disappointment and hurt pride, yes—but both sooner mended. Now Kitty," her mother's honest eyes turned on her. "What are your true feelings towards this man?"

How could Kitty admit that the very sight of him shrivelled her inside into a tight ball of distaste—that the very touch of his hand made her flesh creep. It was impossible to explain the true reason for marrying him, but she couldn't lie either, not to her mother.

"I don't love him. I'll never love anybody but Harvey. I told Adrian so, but he just laughed—" (had it been a laugh, that contemptuous sound from the back of his throat?)—"he said I would grow to love him in time, and that anyway love wasn't the only basis for marriage."

Mrs Tredennick nodded approvingly. "He is right about that—mutual respect is just as important." She allowed a soft sigh to escape her. "But Kitty, you're so young, I hope you know what you're doing. All I want is for you to be happy, my handsome." A pause, then,— "This means you'll be leaving Falmouth, going off to live in London. Try to come back to see us as often as you can."

Kitty choked, her tears flowing afresh. "If you only knew what it means to leave you all—to leave Cornwall—"

"Then why consider it?" her father broke in harshly. His anger had subsided, but not his disappointment. His reaction to Kitty's news had been sparked off as much by the thought that he would lose her as the disclosure of her duplicity. Losing Maggie, good girl though she was, would not have meant sleepless nights, fretting.

Kitty slid out of her chair and went over to him, putting her arms about his neck and resting her head on his shoulder. "Father, I know what you're thinking, but wherever I go, my heart will remain here in Cornwall with you and Mother and Maggie—"

He pushed her away. "Be off with you, puss, you can't get round me like that." Then seeing her puckered face. "There—there if it's what you really want, I won't stand in your way, though I would have respected that shilly-shallying young man a mite more if he'd had the decency to approach me first. Even Harvey did that though he knew in advance what my answer would be. Now girl, I didn't mean to start you off again—you'd best away upstairs and make your peace with your sister."

Kitty left the room without saying another word, but once outside she leant against the closed door, all strength suddenly gone from her limbs. Inside the room her parents were still discussing her. Her father grumbling—her mother pleading. Kitty had no intention of eavesdropping, but too reluctant to face Maggie for a while, she stayed and listened unwittingly.

"Look at it this way, Joe," she heard her mother explaining. "We've seen the way Kitty has been pining. Everywhere she goes in Falmouth recalls memories of Harvey to her. It'll do her good to get away. She's young and she's adaptable and she'll make Adrian a suitable wife, much better than poor Maggie could ever have done. We know our Maggie; a good, dear, reliable girl but she'd be better wed to someone like Dave Williams than to Adrian with his fine connections. Kitty will never disgrace him, but Maggie would have been a fish out of water along with his family. Better it's turned out this way, and it's my dearest wish that one day Maggie will marry Dave. She'd be a fool to let him slip through her fingers."

Her father muttered something Kitty didn't catch, and then she heard the rustle of her mother's skirts as she rose from the table to go to him. Kitty straightened up, lifted her aching head. She couldn't put it off any longer. She must go up to Maggie.

Though it was still daylight outside, the bedroom she shared with Maggie was in semi-darkness. Maggie had pulled down the blinds and drawn the curtains before throwing herself face downwards on the bed. The sight of her huddled body, her boots on the white honeycombe quilt, shook Kitty more than an angry confrontation would have done. It brought home to her the depths of Maggie's despair. There was no sound from her—no movement. "Maggie," she said softly, but there was no answer.

Uncertain how to handle this situation she thought it best to prepare herself for bed. Maggie would have to move then—say something surely? Kitty lit the candle on the washstand, poured out some water into the bowl, then tried to unhook her gown. Maggie and she always helped one another to dress and undress, to brush and braid each other's hair. She found she could not do it on her own. In a burst of misery and frustration she flung herself on the bed beside her sister. "I wish I were dead," she moaned. "Oh how I wish I were dead."

Maggie moved then, but did not turn round. "You might well wish you were dead, you snake in the grass," she said in a stifled voice. "I wish you were dead, too."

Kitty snuggled closer, putting her arm across Maggie's shoulder. "Don't say that, Maggie, I know you don't mean it. I'm going to have a baby—Harvey's baby—that's the only reason I'm marrying Adrian. I'm not very proud of myself. I'm sick to my soul when I allow myself to think what I'm doing because I don't even like Adrian let alone love him. But I can't bring a foundling into the world, and think of the disgrace to Mother and Father. This was my only way out. Oh Maggie, please help me—don't turn away from me—I'm so unhappy."

Even before Kitty's wild cry had subsided Maggie was sitting up and rocking her younger sister in her arms. "Why didn't you tell me? Why have you kept it to yourself? And Harvey—how could he have treated you so—"

But Kitty would hear no criticism of Harvey. Brokenly she told Maggie of that day in April when she and Harvey had sailed to St. Mawes, then walked to Tregorra Cove and married each other in the ruins of the church.

"You baby! You didn't really believe you were legally married, did you?"

"We would have been if we'd been in Scotland, so I don't see why it should be any different down here. In any case we were married in the sight of God, and that's more important than being married in the eyes of the law—I think so, anyway. You believe that too, don't you,

Maggie?"

Maggie sighed in a resigned manner. She looked deeply into Kitty's eyes which glittered feverishly in the candle-light. Secretly she felt that Harvey had taken advantage of a romantic girl's naivety. Yet who was she to judge? Love like this, passionate and unbridled, had never touched her, perhaps it never would. Being completely honest, she knew she had never really cared for Adrian, any more than he had cared for her. During the past month or so it had become more and more obvious with whom his interest lay. Now witnessing what her sister was suffering, seeing the result of a love too heavy to bear, her own hurt began to ease. Kitty had sinned—now she was paying for that sin. She, Maggie, could not add to her misery, but there was one question that had to be asked.

"Adrian—does he know about the baby?"

Kitty shuddered. "I couldn't tell him."

"And you think you can pass Harvey's child off as his? How far gone are you?"

"Nearly three months."

"You little fool, what a risk you are taking. Thin ones like you always show much earlier. Still, if Adrian loves you—" her words were cut off by Kitty placing her hand over her mouth.

"Don't mention love and Adrian in the same sentence."

Maggie wondered at her sister's vehemence. She changed the subject. "When are you to be married?"

"As soon as possible; it will be a very quiet affair—"

"What! None of his grand relations coming?"

Kitty hesitated, choosing her words before answering. "How is it we've built up this idea of grand relations? Adrian has never mentioned any. He has a mother, but she's too frail to make the journey here. We are going to live with her until we find a place of our own."

"And where will that be?"

"Near London, a place called Stratford. Adrian said it was called Stratford-atte-Bower in Chaucer's time—doesn't that sound pretty?" There was such a wistful quality about Kitty's voice that a flood of pity washed over Maggie, and she hugged her sister and kissed her, such an unusual gesture on her part that she immediately drew back, and gave a dry embarrassed cough.

But practical as always, she immediately began to make plans. "I've got a length of very fine navy-blue cashmere put away. I could make that up for you to be married in and I'll make it as full as possible in the skirt. There might be enough material over to make one of those little mantles which are all the rage now and I'll embroider it with beads. It'll be my wedding-present for you." But Kitty didn't want to talk about the wedding anymore. She lay quietly on Maggie's arm, and after a while, when Maggie looked more closely, she saw she had fallen asleep. What a child she still looked—and how in need of protection. An image of Adrian came into her mind and Maggie knew with a sinking heart that whatever Adrian was, the rôle of protector to a high-spirited and in some ways feckless girl, was not one of his functions.

So Kitty was married in the navy-blue cashmere with a small posy of pink moss-roses pinned to the high collar of her mantle. She would not carry a bouquet and refused to allow Maggie to trim her new straw hat with flowers or feathers.

"But you must have some trimming or you'll look as if you're attending your own funeral," remonstrated the scandalized Maggie. Finally she persuaded Kitty to let her decorate the hat with pink satin ribbon.

There was to be a short honeymoon at Penzance, then the newly-weds would travel straight back to London from there. So after a modest reception at Laburnam Road Kitty said goodbye to her parents and sister, dry-eyed and inwardly suffering, but determined not to break down in front of Adrian. At the station she clung to them each in turn, and as the train steamed out of the station she leant out of the window to wave until Adrian dragged her away and pulled up the window with a snap.

When she next travelled on a train, it was three days later, on the overnight express from Penzance to Paddington. This time in a third-class carriage and crowded compartment. The train was steaming out of Plymouth when Kitty wearily opened her eyes. She had feigned sleep to avoid conversation, but it hadn't been necessary. In common with the other passengers Adrian, sitting opposite to her, was sleeping soundly. His head was back, his mouth slightly open, he was snoring faintly. By the dim light of the oil lamps his face looked even more yellow and she looked at him with loathing seeing him as some bestial creature risen from the ashes of her innocence. For she had lost her innocence during the two nights they had spent in the seedy boarding-house in Penzance.

She tried to close her mind to the way Adrian had abused her body; the very memory heightened her colour and sent her heart beating uncomfortably. Even without the comparison to Harvey's gentle and tender love-making she would have been disgusted by Adrian's un-leashed lust. There had been nothing resembling love in his forceful and clumsy handling of her. Love—what a mockery! She shivered, and under cover of her cape placed her hand over her womb. Her one fear was that Adrian's roughness might have harmed the baby. The one thing she looked forward to was its quickening into life—when that happened it would be a surrogate for Harvey.

They pulled into Paddington just before seven a.m. Kitty, who had sat upright and awake all night, had fallen asleep just as dawn was streaking the sky. Now when she opened her eyes, she saw Adrian fully awake and watching her. Her eyes fell before his direct stare; those washed-out protruding eyes, expressionless to an outsider, seemed to her to reflect and distort her most private thoughts. She rose when he did. Their luggage was in the guard's van; his a much-travelled leather portmanteau, hers the new tin trunk which had been a wedding-present from her parents. In that small trunk was everything she possessed. Hidden in it, wrapped in a silk handkerchief, was the ring Harvey had placed on her third finger.

Kitty was overwhelmed by the size of the station and the noise and bustle of steaming trains, doors slamming, whistles blowing. She stayed close to Adrian, frightened of getting separated in the crush, she had never seen so many people together before. Thin-faced ragged boys were everywhere, dodging porters, waylaying travellers—"Carry yer case, mister—get yer a piper, mister."

Adrian sent one of them to buy a copy of *The Morning Post*, and to find out if breakfast was being served in the refreshment room. The urchin came back with the paper and chirping that breakfast was now ready. Adrian gave him a coin which he evidently thought was poor payment for his services, but he pocketed it sullenly. Kitty fell back to ask him what he had been given.

"A bloomin' 'appenny!"

She gave him another penny and was rewarded by a grin that nearly split his peaky little face in two. " 'Cor fanks, mum—lady, I mean. God bless yer and mak' yer 'appy."

It was not a prayer in which she had much faith. Angrily Adrian waited for her. "You will not do that again," he said. "Beggars should not be encouraged."

In Falmouth he had posed as a man of means. They had travelled to Penzance in a reserved first-class compartment, but once in Penzance they had not driven to a hotel as she had supposed but to a boarding house at the back of the town. Their journey to London had been by third-class ticket, now looking about her she saw they were to breakfast in a second-class refreshment-room. It wasn't snobbery on her part that questioned this. Just puzzlement at his double standards. Was it just in front of her parents he had acted the gentleman? Now that he had got what he wanted was he no longer keeping up the charade? For the first time she began to have doubts as to his affluence.

Devoid of lavish decoration the dining-room might be, but the food and service were excellent. Not that Kitty could eat; she made a pretence, crumbling a hot roll on her plate, while Adrian devoured a plate of bacon and eggs and sausages. Afterwards, he arranged for their luggage to be sent on by carrier, then led her to the forecourt of the station where Kitty expected him to hail one of the waiting cabs, but still part leading, part pushing her through the early morning rush of travellers, they came out to the main thoroughfare.

It was Kitty's first sight of a busy London street, and instinctively she recoiled. She had never seen so many horses before, so many carts and carriages, cabs and omnibuses—they were packed together into a solid mass of moving horse-flesh and vehicles and the noise was deafening. It was impossible to see across to the opposite side of the street and the pungent smell of horse dung made her feel faint.

Adrian raised his cane and stopped a passing omnibus. It was a new experience for Kitty to ride on a horse-bus but by now she was too weary and too bewildered to take much note. It was only a short journey and the whole time she sat and stared at a notice forbidding spitting.

They alighted at another railway terminus, Liverpool Street, even more cavernous it seemed to Kitty than Paddington. They had exchanged the Great Western Railway for the Great Eastern. "Surely we are not going on another train?" She could have wept from sheer fatigue.

"Just a short train ride this time," Adrian remarked curtly. He too was showing signs of fatigue. His eyes were puffy and his unhealthy pallor more marked. They boarded a train which had just disgorged its passengers— mostly men, all soberly dressed, all with the same peaked, strained expression. The thing that had struck Kitty most on her short ride across London was the dull look of its people, and their complexions like cotton wool, she thought.

Adrian and herself seemed to be the only ones going away from London, at least they had a compartment to themselves. It was very bare and comfortless with wooden walls that did not reach to the ceiling. She heard someone get into the compartment next to theirs and a head appeared over the partition and stared with curious eyes at Kitty. Only when Adrian coughed noisily did the head subside but not before its owner, raising his battered bowler, treated Kitty to a bawdy grin.

"The man's drunk. You shouldn't have encouraged him," said Adrian shortly.

"I didn't say a word."

"You didn't have to. It's the way you have of looking under your lashes. You'll have to curb that habit."

Adrian settled to his newspaper. Kitty stared unhappily out of the window. The train plunged into a network of tunnels and when it emerged into daylight again she was confronted by a scene of devastating squalor and poverty. Warehouses and factories alternated with human rookeries from which grey and tattered washing hung like flags at half-mast. She found it hard to believe that people actually lived in such dwellings. There were poor people's homes in Falmouth, but nothing to equal this. She was amazed at the hundreds of chimney-pots all belching smoke. The brickwork of the factories and houses was black with soot. Men, women and children lived here—breathed this atmosphere—perhaps they had never known it otherwise. She thought of the stinging salt spray blowing in on the wind off the sea at Falmouth and wondered if she would ever learn to adapt to a different environment. Would she in time lose her golden tan? But she had lost so much already it seemed a small thing to grieve about.

It worried her that through force of circumstance, people had to live like this. She ached to see green lawns and trees, not these narrow, blackened yards which passed as gardens. But they had hardly got clear of the grimy rookeries before they were running past shunting yards and engine sheds and the train began to slow down. Adrian folded his paper and put it in his pocket. He stood up.

"We surely haven't arrived!"

"Why do you always have to put your statements in the form of a question," he said testily. "Yes, we have arrived and we have quite a walk before us too."

There was no bustling activity in the station forecourt here. Just a coal-cart with a tired-looking nag between its shafts and a stout woman in rusty black sitting beside her flower basket, her head nodding in sleep.

So this was Stratford. Stratford-atte-Bower—such a pretty name she had told Maggie. She could well imagine Maggie's retort if she were here now. Where was the bower in this network of mean streets?

Yet Stratford had its gracious features. The wide cobbled market square, the neo-Gothic church half-hidden among trees, the fine modern shops with plate-glass windows in the Broadway. It was the back streets through which they were threading which so depressed her. Adrian walked with short fussy steps pointing his toes inwards, but covering the ground with incredible speed. She was too weary to keep up with him or to wonder whether they were taking a short cut. Why else should they go down one dull street after another? They turned into one called Milton Street and the only thing to mark it out from its neighbours was the shabby little shop on the corner.

Adrian stopped by the shop to wait for her. Kitty gazed at it without interest. There were such shops even in Falmouth, drapers and haberdashers of the more modest kind. A small hand-written card pasted in the corner of the window advertised—'Alterations and Repairs undertaken on the premises.'

To her surprise Adrian opened the shop door and went in. The ping of its bell brought the proprietress from the back parlour. She was a thin, round-shouldered woman in her early sixties, neat and clean in appearance but impregnated with an overall impression of drabness. When she looked up with hostile, protuberant eyes, Kitty felt as if a drop of icy water had trickled down her back.

"Mother," said Adrian, "this is Kitty, my wife. Kitty—my mother."

FOUR

Kitty sat at the washstand in her bedroom trying to answer a letter from Maggie. She was using the wash-stand as a desk, not from choice, but because the only alternative was the table in the shop-parlour under the watchful eye of her mother-in-law. The sitting-room above the shop was used only on Sundays.

Maggie's letter to her was a week old and had been read so many times that the paper was beginning to split along the folds. Kitty fancied that a whiff of sea air escaped from the pages each time she undid them. She opened the letter again now. Maggie had a good hand; she wrote in the long Italianate style she had been taught at school. But the content of the letter had little in common with the delicacy of its script.

—"Are you so busy carousing that you have no time to

write us a proper letter? We have received nothing but a brief note to say you had arrived at Stratford—since then no a word in three weeks. I suppose you are still on your honeymoon" (was Maggie being ironic!) "but won't you spare a thought for Mother; she is too weak to write to you herself. The doctor says it is only a tired heart, but I feel she is fretting for you. She lies patiently in bed, living from one post to the next. Write something, anything— just to show that you still care, and that you don't now consider us your unimportant poor relations—"

This last sentence always brought stinging tears to Kitty's eyes. She brushed them away with the palm of her hand. "Oh Maggie, if you only knew." She conjured up an image of her sister. The broad face, the widely-spaced round eyes completely devoid of guile, the plump hands so gentle and always cool. With all her heart she wanted her family to know of her true circumstances, but that was an indulgence she must forego. She loved them too much to add concern for herself to their other worries.

But sitting there idly in the fustiness of the over-furnished and airless room she allowed her imagination to weave the words she could never commit to paper.

'Dearest Maggie,

Do you really want to know what my life is really like? Would you care to learn of the fate you so happily escaped? I have been trapped, my dear sister, I have been trapped as neatly as in turn I trapped my husband. We are deceivers both, so I'm in no position to complain, am I?

'My home is not grand. I have no servants, no carriage, as you seem to think. It is not even my own home, but a humble little shop owned by my mother-in-law who dislikes me as much as I dislike her. I have seen more poverty and hardship around me here than I guessed possible. Fresh air is at a premium—less important to me is lack of money. Perhaps my husband feels that as he feeds and houses me benevolence can go no further. He

42

is as mean as he is brutal. My longing for Cornwall and the sight of dear, familiar faces makes each day more unbearable. On my first evening here I overheard my mother-in-law say;—'You must have been mad marrying a penniless little chit like that—you with your prospects.' What his prospects are remain a mystery. There has been no further mention of moving to a home of our own, and I can't believe that this shop is the sole means of our support.

'A week after we arrived my husband donned his best suit and went off for the day. He is out every day except Sunday, and on Tuesdays he is never home before midnight. I presume he is working somewhere. He doesn't confide in me and I never speak unless spoken to first—'

Kitty slumped back in her chair. Even in imagination the sardonic tone of her pretence ould not be sustained. Her homesickness and despair were too deep-seated for that kind of levity. There were so many things she could not explain to Maggie. The enigma that was Adrian was one. He still followed her every movement with his pale cold eyes. Nothing would convince her that what he felt for her was love. Why had he married her? Because he could not get her any other way? Her mind shied away from reflecting on the nightly loveless ritual. She knew that nothing annoyed him more than the passive acceptance of her circumstances. He had once remarked that he would like nothing better than the taming of her, so she made sure that there would be nothing in her behaviour requiring taming. It cost a lot to keep her wilful spirit in control, but she knew it would cost her a lot more to reveal her true feelings and give Adrian the chance he wanted.

She could not be sure whether it was indifference or just pure thoughtlessness to keep her shut up in the shop premises day after day in the inescapable heat. Never once had he offered to take her out and her pride would not allow her to ask favours of him. Once she had ventured on her own as far as the Broadway to look in the shop windows, and she sometimes went on small errands to the market in Angel Lane, but she didn't consider these as outings and, in any case, Stratford depressed her.

She longed for the sound of the sea, to hear the cry of seagulls, to see them wheeling and banking in the wake of the incoming ships. More than anything she longed for Falmouth, for its crowded harbour and tanned robust people and the magnificent sight of the training ship *Ganges* riding at anchor in Carrick Roads.

Once, in desperation, she asked to help in the shop—anything to help the tedium of the long, lonely hours—but had been curtly rejected. "Perhaps the old termagant thinks I might help myself from the till," Kitty wondered. Then she had suggested she took on some of the alterations, but when she admitted that she did not know how to use a machine, was again rebuffed.

The days were long enough, but the evenings were worst. They were spent in the parlour behind the shop. It smelt of cigar-smoke and grease. Adrian buried himself behind his paper; Mrs Beatty worked away at her treadle, and Kitty had nothing better to do than listen to the popping of the gas-mantle.

Her greatest privation next to that of fresh air was the lack of good nourishing food. Adrian ate most of his meals out, and his mother seemed to exist on bread and butter and weak tea. Kitty tried to suppress memories of her mother's rich pasties filled with meat and potatoes and onion or the clotted cream they always had with scones and jam on Sundays. Best of all, the lobsters that 'Old Jake', her father's oldest employee, would bring along to Laburnum Road as a peace-offering after an unofficial day off work from a too liberal 'bending of his elbow' as her father would say.

One tea-time the bread was so dry she didn't attempt to eat it. Mrs Beatty fixed her with her fish-like eyes. "What's wrong?"

"The bread's too hard."

"It'd be harder still if there wasn't any." Kitty felt her mother-in-law had been saving that remark just for such a moment as this. She didn't begrudge her her petty triumph until supper-time when the bread reappeared. This time Mrs Beatty crumpled it into a bowl, added hot milk, sugar and a knob of butter and proceeded to eat it with exaggerated relish. She didn't offer any to Kitty.

Kitty had always had a healthy appetite and now in 'old wives' parlance she was eating for two. The sweet nutty smell of the bread-and-milk recalled the times it had been used as a panacea for tempting small appetites after childish disorders. At home though, it had been made with rich farm butter and milk the colour of cream. Kitty could never get used to the bluey-white milk that appeared on Mrs Beatty's table. She couldn't be sure whether it was the milkman or her mother-in-law who watered it down. She suspected the latter.

After going supperless to bed that night, Kitty never again criticized what was put before her and even ate her way through a boiled egg which wasn't quite fresh and made her gorge rise with every mouthful. If she had had the money she would have treated herself to something from the German baker's in the next street, but all she had left was a few shillings from the small sum she had brought from Falmouth, and this she hoarded like a miser.

And now she sat at the washstand, twisting her pen in her fingers, unable to write the truth and not dishonest enough to invent lies. Her eyes wandered abstractedly around the room. It was still a man's room, her presence hadn't altered it one jot. There was no dressing-table.

Only a marble-topped tallboy on which Adrian kept his shaving things, a pair of silver-backed hair brushes and the bay-rum with which he liberally pomaded his hair. Kitty kept her own comb and brush on the mantelpiece, though Adrian had made room for her. She avoided any contact with his possessions, but from expediency had to share the wardrobe with him though her clothes took up pitifully little room. She had only three dresses. The navy-blue cashmere in which she had been married, the black lawn which had been Maggie's, and also the white muslin that Maggie had worn at the ill-fated Jubilee Ball.

At first, Kitty had refused this last gift, but Maggie had insisted. "You can return it to me when Adrian buys you some new clothes, but you must have one cool dress in this hot weather."

All through the '80's, the summer days had been fierce and cloudless. In the cramped living space of the shop no air stirred at all, and Kitty wore the white muslin daily, laundering it herself, once a week. When she did go out she wore the grey alpaca mantle which had belonged to her mother and which Maggie had made over for her. It was out of fashion now, but here, in East London, fashion as a word meant little. The difference lay between rags and clothes.

There were still some large houses around, an inheritance from Stratford's more prosperous era when wealthy merchants moved out from Whitechapel Road to the country lanes further east. But then the railways had arrived to cut a swathe through the green fields, leaving a way open for the speculators to fill in the gaps with rows of working-class cottages. The large houses that remained hid behind high walls topped with broken glass to keep out intruders. Their owners were rarely seen on the pavements. When they went abroad it was in their own carriages.

All this Kitty could have put in a letter to Maggie, but to

what avail? Unhappiness shared feeds on itself—it doesn't lighten, so she tore up the letter that had got no further than—'Dearest Maggie'—and began to pace up and down the room. She felt perspiration running down between her shoulder blades. The sun had reached the narrow window and was drawing up the smells she associated with Adrian—leather, bay-rum, cigar-smoke, stale perspiration. She pushed the window up as high as it would go, and was immediately assailed by the smell of the near-by brewery. She felt her stomach churn with nausea, so she closed it again.

She had to get out of this fusty trap. She put on her mantle and hat and went downstairs. She could hear her mother-in-law talking to a customer in the shop so she let herself out of the back door and through the yard.

When she reached the Broadway and saw a tram lumbering towards her she acted on a sudden impulse and stopped it and asked the conductor whether it was going anywhere near open country.

Fortunately for her he was a sympathetic man. "Not this one, luv, we're jest off to the depot. Open country, eh? Your best bet is Chingford Plains. You don't know 'em? Then you better take the train. You may 'ave to change at Bethnal Green; they'll tell you at the station."

Bethnal Green—that was a misnomer. Kitty glimpsed nothing but tenements and chimney pots. Her heart sank. Would Chingford Plains turn out to be another disappointment? She was prepared for this, so was delighted when she stepped out of the station to see rolling grassland stretching for miles, and on the horizon trees shaded from lime to olive, a serrated wall of green against the sky. It was such a feast of colour and space and out-doorness that she could have cried aloud with delight. After weeks of being closeted in dingy streets the wide open spaciousness filled her with a sense of exhilaration.

"Buy a flower, luv. Buy a pretty flower." It was the

47

inevitable flower-girl—though this 'girl' was nearer sixty. The only other person in sight was the driver of the station fly, a stout man in a bowler hat. He was dozing on his seat, and his horse, tormented by flies, jingled its harness. The man opened one eye at Kitty, but as she did not beckon to him, nodded off again. Kitty approached the flower-seller.

"Could you tell me—is all that grass private, or can anybody walk on it?"

The woman grinned exposing broken teeth. "You ain't never 'eard of Epping Forest? No, I don't s'pose you 'ave, not with that accent. You don't come from these parts? Them's Chingford Plains, dearie, an' no, they're not private—leastways not now. They look quiet enough now, don't they? You should've seen them last Monday— Bank 'Oliday Monday." A deep-throated chuckle. "You'd 'ave been 'ard put to see a blade of grass between all the people there then. They just poured outer the trains—every ten minutes—I wondered they even found standing room. Plenty of company I 'ad 'ere in the yard. Whelk stalls and sweet stalls selling rock, and another chap selling balloons an' streamers. Every one making for the Fair. There's bin a Fair on Chingford Plains every Bank 'Oliday ever since there's bin Bank 'Olidays, an' that nigh on twenty years, an' I can remember fairs 'ere before that even." Her voice suddenly resumed its professional whine. "Buy a pretty flower, dear, I 'aven't done much business since last week. 'Ere, I'll let you 'ave a bunch of lavender for a penny, that's 'alf wot it's worth."

It was a penny she could ill-afford and the lavender was wilting in the sun; but Harvey used to wear a sprig of lavender in his button-hole when it was in bloom, so she buried her nose in it and tried to revive scents of happier times.

The Plains were fascinating. There were few people about. In the distance she could see two men playing golf.

She enjoyed walking on the grass feeling the rough turf springing back under her boots. There were many ditches to jump and parts of the Plain were corrugated with green furrows as if centuries before it had been under the plough. She reached the tree line and plunged into the deep shade, completely unaware she was in a primeval forest. The bracken was as high as her waist. She pretended it was the sea and pushed against it as against Atlantic rollers, reliving for a brief few moments her happy childhood. When finally she came to a clearing she was glad to sit down and rest. There were anthills as high as chairs and rabbit droppings littered the ground like dried currants. She was unfamiliar with many of the trees which ringed her, but she recognized silver birch and holly and the oak-trees were enormous. Bees were busy in the undergrowth and the bracken had a hot spicy aroma that acted like a narcotic. She unlaced her boots, laid back and was soon asleep.

She was awakened by someone shaking her. A middle-aged man, lean-faced, with a waxed moustache leaned over her. "Are you all right, miss?"

He helped her to her feet. She blinked at him stupidly, taking some while to recall her surroundings. "Good gracious, I fell asleep. Whatever is the time?"

"Three o'clock, miss—ma'am." He had noticed her wedding-ring as she hastily fastened her boots. "I'm sorry if I startled you. I'm a forest keeper; I thought at first you might be unwell."

"Am I trespassing?"

He smiled thinly. "Indeed not, ma'am. This forest was presented to the public five years ago when Her Majesty herself came to Chingford for the ceremony. A grand occasion that was."

"Who owned it before then?"

"Well I reckon anybody with a little bit of power could carve himself off a bit anytime he liked—many did, and

49

any Tom, Dick or Harry could graze their cattle on it and lop the trees for firewood. That's why they have us keepers. We have to keep an eye out for that sort of thing—besides others."

She saw then he was in uniform of a sort—velveteen jacket and leather gaiters. There was a military bearing about him as if he had once been in the army. He escorted her back across the Plains and put her on the bus for Chingford Mount, from where she would then be able to catch a tram to Stratford.

If he was puzzled as to why she should be wandering in the forest on her own, it did not show on his impassive countenance. Some women he would have seen off with scant courtesy, but he could tell she wasn't of that genre. Kitty alighted from the tram at Stratford faint with hunger. If it hadn't been for the anxiety of the forest keeper to see her safely on her way she would have looked for a café in Chingford. She has missed dinner; out of pique Mrs Beatty was quite capable of withholding tea. She hesitated outside a jellied eel and pie-shop. She had never been inside one but the smell that drifted on to the pavement made her mouth water. Looking in, however, she saw it was occupied chiefly by men and her courage failed her, then she remembered a pork butcher's on the next corner.

The woman behind the counter asked for a basin when Kitty ordered a slice of hot pork and twopennyworth of pease-pudding, and 'tched-tched' impatiently when Kitty had to admit she had not brought a container. Nevertheless she cut off a thick slice of fat pork, liberally spread it with the steaming pease-pudding and wrapped the whole in newspaper.

Kitty had nothing to eat with but her fingers, but she was too hungry to care. Who would take notice anyway?— nobody knew her here. All the same, she walked furtively, her head lowered while she crammed the food into her mouth. She didn't care if she was awake all night with heart-burn, for the first time in weeks she was going to bed satiated. Suddenly she began to laugh, laughter mixed with bitter tears.

If only Maggie could see her now—Maggie with her false idea of her little sister's new-found grandeur. What would she make of the banquet Kitty was enjoying?

FIVE

Kitty went straight upstairs to her room. She badly needed a wash, her hands were greasy from the pork. She saw that her gown was marked with grass stains and the hem was black with grime. She hadn't realized in her ecstasy of seeing trees and grass again that over all was laid a veneer of soot blown on the wind from the factory chimneys of the East End. She didn't stop to change after freshening herself up, she was dying for a cup of tea.

She could hear Mrs Beatty in the shop. She went through the parlour into the scullery which she avoided as much as possible—for it was as dank as it smelled—and made a pot of tea.

It was while she was putting the cup and saucer away afterwards that she first saw the telegram propped against the clock on the mantelpiece. It was addressed to herself and had been opened.

She snatched at it. It was from Maggie, who had wasted no words—'Come at once. Mother dying.'

Kitty didn't hear Mrs Beatty come into the parlour, didn't know she was behind her until her flat voice broke the silence. "If you hadn't gone off skulking the way you did, you would have got your bad news before this."

Kitty turned on her like a tigress. "You opened my telegram!"

"Of course I did—it might have needed an answer. The boy waited." Ther was no word of condolence, no compassion in her voice.

"My mother is dying—dying—" Kitty's voice rose in panic; "and I won't be able to get to her in time, I know I won't." She dashed out of the room and up the stairs tearing off the muslin dress as she ran. She went through the actions of changing and dressing like an automaton, thinking only of ways and means of getting to Falmouth. She didn't stop to pack, Maggie would lend her anything she needed. She hurried downstairs, and there was Mrs Beatty waiting for her in the narrow hall.

"And where do you think you're off to?"

"To telegraph my sister, and then to Paddington of course—"

"You're not thinking to going to Cornwall this evening!"

"Just as soon as I possibly can."

Mrs Beatty's pale eyes flickered with annoyance. "Stop behaving like a hysterical shop-girl; pull yourself together. You can't do anything tonight. Wait until your husband comes home, then ask his advice."

"It's Tuesday. You know he won't be home before midnight, by that time I would have missed the last train to Falmouth."

"And what do you intend to use for money?"

Kitty looked at her mother-in-law with contempt. So

she knew her son kept his wife short of money. Was it a deliberate ploy on both their parts? But what did that matter now. Kitty swallowed her pride. "Will you lend me the money for my fare?" she asked without any hope.

"I certainly will not. I know Adrian will not approve of money being thrown away on a useless gesture. You said yourself you would not get to your mother in time. Also, considering your condition, I don't think it right for you to go careering off on your own."

"My—my condition—" Kitty echoed lamely.

"You don't think you can fool me, do you, girl? I've heard you retching your insides out every morning in the water-closet; my bedroom's in the back, remember. It finally made sense to me why my son had been trapped into marrying you. He's an honourable man and would do his duty, though to be sure, you must have egged him on in the first place—"

But Kitty wouldn't stop to hear more. The whining, accusing voice followed her out into the street. Normally Mrs Beatty did not have much to say to her, but today she had found her voice with a vengeance and her pent-up resentment and spite underlined every word she uttered. At any other time Kitty would have been distressed to think she was hated so, for until recently she had been loved and petted by everybody who knew her; but only one thought was uppermost in her mind now—her mother was dying—and she had to get to her somehow.

She telegraphed to Maggie, then stood outside the post office, twisitng her gloves in her hands, wondering how to raise the money for her fare. Across the road was a pawn-shop. Early every Monday morning before it opened a queue of women would form, their husband's Sunday suits in bundles under their arms. The few coppers these realized would eke out the expenses until pay-day on the following Saturday, then the suits would be redeemed, worn for the day of rest and then pawned

54

again on the Monday.

But there was no queue now. Kitty gathered up her skirt in one hand and crossed the road where the crossing-sweeper had made a path amidst the dust and dung. A pawnbroker was a new experience to Kitty, but she did not hesitate. Wordlessly she slipped off her wedding-ring and placed it on the counter.

The pawnbroker wore pince-nez and he looked over the top of these at Kitty with solemn eyes. She felt that she was under a microscope. He studied the ring casually, then shook his head.

"I'm afraid this is only nine-carat gold. I could only let you have a shilling or two on it."

How like Adrian to have bought her with the cheapest possible ring! She thought of the other ring, that was now secreted in her handbag—the ring that had belonged to Harvey's mother. She was having a bitter struggle between her longing to keep it and an equal longing to go to her mother when the pawnbroker said; "I could lend you two guineas on that brooch you are wearing."

Two guineas! That would more than pay her fare. With trembling fingers she undid the brooch that only as a last thought had she pinned to her collar.

"A beautiful piece of carving," said the pawnbroker, caressing the cameo with long thin fingers. Again he quizzed Kitty over the top of his pince-nez, this time his eyes smiling. "And not long to stay in my possession, eh?"

"Indeed no, I shall be back to redeem it as soon as I can. You will keep it for me, won't you?"

His smile spread to his lips, and he assured her on that point. Kitty picked up the two sovereigns and a florin he placed on the counter and put them in her purse. She had the means—now for the ways.

She had a long wait at Paddington Station. The next train to Falmouth wasn't leaving until nine o'clock, and was due in at seven-thirty the following morning. If she had not given in to that irresponsible impulse to seek green fields and open spaces, she would have received Maggie's telegram that morning and been in time to catch the noon-day train. What had happened to her mother in those long wasted hours? She would not dwell on such thoughts—it wouldn't help her reach her mother any the quicker. When at last the west-bound train steamed out of Paddington, she was so racked by mental and physical anguish that once she was seated, she fell into a deep and dreamless sleep.

Maggie was waiting for her at Falmouth station, the early-morning sun highlighting the reddened skin about her eyes. They went into each other's arms, and Kitty began to sob. There was no need for questions—Maggie's face said it all.

"When?" Kitty managed at last, blowing her nose then straightening her hat.

"Yesterday evening, just after your telegram came. That gave her comfort."

It was of some comfort to Kitty too to know that her mother had understood that she was coming to see her. "Tell me, Maggie—it wasn't my fault she died—fretting about me, I mean?"

"Oh no; it was her heart. There wasn't much we could do but spare her worry. But why didn't you write? A letter from you would have meant so much to her."

Kitty gave a deep sigh. "If you only knew why, but I can't tell you now, Maggie; later perhaps. How's Father?"

"Taking it very badly. The shock of Mother's death coming so soon after the collapse of his business seems to have unhinged his mind." Maggie spoke drearily, as if it were a speech she had repeated many times before.

They were climbing the hill from the station, a milk-white mist hung low over the sea, muffling the cry of the gulls. Kitty stopped and pulled at her sister's arm. "What do you mean—the collapse of the business? Not the boatyard?"

Maggie freed her arm and trudged onwards. She spoke bitterly; "Oh come, it isn't all that long since you left, and you knew how things were then. The boatyard has been failing for months—ever since Harvey left in fact, and goodness knows it wasn't doing too well even then. After—after the funeral, Father will be looking for a job. We'll have to leave Laburnum Road. We only stayed on for Mother's sake."

Leave Laburnum Road—the place she looked upon as home—it seemed inconceivable. "Where will you go?" she asked dully.

"Dave knows of a vacant cottage near the harbour. It's very small—but then so is the rent, and that's the main thing. Kitty, you don't know how lucky you are to have got away from all this."

Kitty threw her sister a quick, sideways look. Was the guileless Maggie being ironic? But no, she could see by her expression that Maggie had spoken quite innocently. Why should she think otherwise? For her, things in general were either white or black; she had no idea of the murky shades of grey in between.

For her part Maggie had been surreptitiously eyeing Kitty's navy-blue dress. She thought it odd that Kitty should be still wearing the same attire in which she had been married. Surely Adrian must have bought her something more suitable for the hot weather. But perhaps Kitty had thought a dark dress more appropriate for the occasion. Her gaze continued upwards noting the unusual pallor of her sister's face, the lines of weariness etched about the curved mouth.

"How pale and thin you look, Kitty," she said tenderly. "I had forgotten your condition for the moment. You must be worn out and starving after your journey."

57

"I had a cup of tea and some toast at Truro—there was time between trains. I'm not hungry, honestly, but I could do with a lie-down."

"And so you shall after—after you've seen Mother—"

The undertaker had called during Maggie's absence. Ada Tredennick lay in her coffin in the front parlour. In death she looked younger and out of pain.

But Kitty looking down at her through a blur of tears could not recognize her mother lying there. Her hair had been carefully coiffured and her arms were crossed over her breast; she looked at peace, but she also looked a stranger. You are just a receptacle—a shell, thought Kitty with anguish. The essential part of her mother; her voice—her smile—that was gone. What remained made mockery of the warm, living being she had come hundreds of miles to see.

The appearance of her father was another shock. In the few weeks since she had last seen him he had aged years. He kissed her in an absent-minded way and enquired after her health, then returned to his place of guardianship beside the remains of his wife. Kitty, feeling that she was intruding on his private grief, allowed Maggie to help her up the stairs to their old room.

The years slipped away—she could have been five again as Maggie, her older sister, gently took off her outer clothing and, pulling off the bedspread and blankets, tucked her in between the sheets. Methodically she shook out the cashmere dress and mantle and gave them a good brush before hanging them in the wardrobe. The sun was streaming onto the bed. She pulled down the blind, then damping her face flannel in the pitcher, she laid it across Kitty's forehead.

"How does that feel?"

"Marvellous." Kitty closed her eyes. "You always know just what to do, Maggie."

"I wish I did! I'm worried about you, Kitty. There's

something wrong, I can sense it. Why didn't you write?"

A great longing to confide in her came over Kitty, and out it all came in a torrent of words—all the little humiliations and frustrations of the past weeks. She only spared Maggie the more intimate details of her married life. That was something she could not talk about, but she described in detail the sordidness of the shabby back-street shop and the pettiness and meanness of her mother-in-law not caring in her mood of released tension whether she stuck strictly to the truth or not.

It was too incomprehensible to Maggie. "But where does Adrian get all his money from if, as you say, the shop isn't paying its way?"

"I don't know that it's 'all that money'—I haven't seen much of it. I believe he works—after a fashion, and at hours to suit himself. But he has never told me and I wouldn't demean myself to ask."

"Do you hate him so much, Kitty?"

Kitty pondered that question. "No, I don't hate him. I wouldn't waste such a strong emotion as hatred on him—he isn't worth it."

Maggie looked even more distressed. "Oh, Kitty—Kitty—I've never seen you like this before—what has happened to you. Do you fear him?"

"No—not physically, anyway. But I know he would love to break my spirit—have me crawling at his feet for mercy. If I did get that near to his feet I'd bite a lump out of them!"

Maggie let out a bellow of laughter, remembered her mother, and clapped her hand to her mouth. "That's more like my old Kitty," she said, wiping her eyes, for her laughter had turned quickly to tears. "I didn't like the look on your face just now. It was—well, sinister." She went over to the dressing-table and began to fiddle with the trinkets on it. "Supposing I had married Adrian; do you think he would have treated me the same?"

Kitty pulled herself into a sitting position and twined her arms around her knees. She lowered her chin and looked fondly across at her sister. "But Maggie dear, he never intended marrying you. It was me he was after, all the time. He didn't love me; he lusted after me, and the more I resisted him the more he desired me—" she stopped, seeing Maggie's embarrassment. She could never make her understand without being more explicit, and she wanted to spare Maggie that. It occurred to her that their rôles had become reversed. She was the older now, made so by experience; perhaps, one day when Maggie was married herself, she'd be able to confide in her, but as things were now—she shrugged off her feeling of hopelessness and got out of bed. Maggie was standing half-turned away from her, biting her lip. Kitty put her head on the other's firm shoulder.

"I couldn't write feeling like I did. If I could have unburdened myself, yes—I would have done. But knowing Mother was unwell—causing you fresh worry—it would have been so selfish of me. I kept remembering the promise I made to send you money, but I just didn't have any to send. I even had to pawn grandmother's brooch to raise the money to get here."

Maggie shook her head as if it were all beyond her. There were still signs of tears on her cheeks, and her underlip trembled. "All I can think is, thank God Mother is dead—this would have broken her heart; she thought you had done so well for yourself." She saw nothing illogical about her words. "So that's why you're wearing your wedding dress. I suppose you have nothing else?"

"The white muslin and the black lawn that were both yours, and I didn't stop to pack them."

"Well there's a black skirt and a black satin blouse that were Mother's that I can alter for you for the funeral. But surely Adrian would telegraph you some money if he knew the circumstances—"

Kitty stopped her by gently placing two fingers against her lips. "Darling Maggie, try to understand. I wouldn't ask him for a farthing—I wouldn't give him the satisfaction."

The day following the funeral the two sisters went for a walk as far as Gyllyngvase Beach. The scorching sun was tempered by a mild on-shore breeze which brought with it too the tempting aroma of spices from a ship unloading in harbour. The girls eased themselves onto the sands, baking under the sun's glare. Their nearest neighbours were over a hundred yards away; two small children jumping the waves under the watchful eye of their nurse. Maggie followed Kitty's gaze.

"D'you remember when we used to do that? We would come here to picnic with Mother and Father, and Mother would make one of her enormous pasties and we'd bathe in our chemises. That was only twelve years ago, Kitty. But things were so different then; we had enough money—a servant—no inkling of the future. Fancy you having to wear Mother's old blouse and skirt at her own funeral, and I couldn't even afford crêpe—"

Maggie was on the point of breaking down again. Kitty hugged her. "Don't talk about the past, don't even think about it. If you start crying it'll only set me off, and all I seem to do lately is cry, and you know what they say about expectant mothers crying? That they'll have fretful babies."

Kitty couldn't have made a more pertinent appeal. Maggie responded at once, thinking only of her sister's well-being. Their conversation turned to more practical matters. Kitty asked what plans Maggie and their father had made for the future. "That depends on Dave," Maggie said laconically.

When pressed, she added; "On whether he still wants to marry me. It would solve our immediate problem. We'd not be very well off, but we wouldn't be so dismally

61

poor as Father and I on our own."

"You mean you'd marry Dave, without loving him, just for security?"

"You're a fine one to talk about a loveless marriage. And who said I didn't love Dave? I do—after a fashion."

Kitty was hurt by Maggie's words, and felt tears pricking her eyelids. She began to play with the sand letting it trickle through her fingers. Maggie watched as if mesmerised.

"Everything's turned out so differently from what Mother planned for us, hasn't it, Kitty? I was to marry a master mariner and have a large family. And you—oh, there had to be someone very special for you. Poor Mother's imagination fell short when planning for you. Fine prospects we both have now!"

Kitty straightened her back. Having no support it ached. Her stays were digging into her just below the breasts; she'd snip the whalebone before wearing them again. "We agreed not to talk about the past," she said, "but as you've brought it up again, what did you mean by saying that the boatyard began to fail as soon as Harvey left?"

"Perhaps you were too young to remember when Harvey first started—Father said he was like a fresh wind blowing away the cobwebs. He had initiative—new ideas—but more importantly he had connections—his father's old cronies. Orders started to roll in. It gave the business a new lease of life, but when Harvey left the customers left too, went to more flourishing places. Father just couldn't compete." Maggie turned reproachful eyes on her sister. "Don't you ever feel any resentment towards Harvey? I mean, taking it into his head to dash off to America like that. Why America? There's work for the asking in the new shipyards of the North. With his flair for design he would soon have made good. If you want to know what I think, it wasn't a fortune he

62

was after—it was adventure. He was always a restless one."

Kitty drooped her head and suddenly the tears gushed out—the tears she had stemmed at her mother's funeral worrying about their effect on her baby. Full of contrition Maggie cradled her. "Dear Kitty, I should be ashamed of myself. I've got you for such a short time and I'm nearly quarelling with you. Come on—let's go home and have tea. I'll bake some pilchards. D'you remember that song Dave taught you about pilchards, do you still remember the words?"

"Yes, but I've forgotten how to sing."

"You'll sing again one day, when you're happy again."

Kitty stayed three days more at Falmouth, and in spite of her gnawing grief and fears of the future, those days proved very sweet. There were no more recriminations between herself and Maggie and they drew closer than ever. That afternoon on the sands had acted like a restorative to their spirits. There was much to be done. Their mother's personal effects to be sorted out and furniture to be docketed and stored. Their father was no help, he took little interest in what was going on around him, but Dave hovered patiently in the background, never intruding but always at hand when needed.

It was he who paid for Kitty's return fare to Paddington, saying in his shy way that if it made her feel better she could look upon it as a loan. He offered to go with Maggie to the station to see her off, but Maggie wouldn't have that, saying she wanted the last few moments with Kitty alone. Yet when that time came they had little to say to each other, or too much to encompass in such a short time. In Kitty's bag was a small package Maggie had given her the evening before. It contained five sovereigns. At first Kitty had refused the gift but Maggie had been adamant. "It's my own to give, from my savings. Look upon it as a present for the baby—you'll need it when the time comes. And here is a parcel of some of Mother's clothes. I've altered them as best as I can. They may come in useful."

Now in the same no-nonsense voice Maggie was saying; "You have your sandwiches? Is your ticket handy? What time do you expect to get to London?"

"Just after nine o'clock—"

"It'll be dark by then. I don't like the idea of you being alone in London after dark. I'd better telegraph Adrian."

"I'd rather you didn't. I can catch a cab to Liverpool Street. I feel quite wealthy now," Kitty's laugh turned into a sob.

Maggie grabbed her and kissed her fiercely. "Write to me," she commanded. "Write anything, but write!"

Kitty's train steamed into Paddington just before nine o'clock. She was stiff from sitting so long and longing to get to the Ladies' Room to loosen her stays. She had eaten her sandwiches, but had had nothing to drink. She was shy of going into the crowded refreshment-room on her own, and much to her relief spotted a white-aproned boy with a tea-waggon. High above her, pigeons roosting in the glass-filled vaulted roof kept up a ceaseless susurration constantly interrupted by the arrival and departure of the trains. The noise and the turmoil all about her made her head throb and she longed for bed, but bed also meant Adrian, and her mind flinched, remembering.

There had been a heavy downpour of rain during the journey and the London pavements were still wet. When she alighted from the train at Stratford it had settled down to a steady drizzle. There was usually a four-wheeled cab waiting in the yard and she was relieved to see it was still there, the tired old horse standing with legs splayed, patient and unmoving, rain dripping from its flanks. And then suddenly she saw Adrian, standing by the cab saying; "Come, I have been waiting."

Maggie must have telegraphed him after all. She was

64

too weary to resist when he took her arm and helped her into the cab. It was very dirty and the straw on the floor hadn't been changed for days. It smelled mouldy, but it was better than walking. She wouldn't have had the strength to put one foot before the other.

At Milton Street Adrian helped her to alight. He hadn't spoken a word during the short journey. He paid off the cabby and they entered the shop. In the narrow passage Mrs Beatty was waiting, a slight, dark figure in the gas-light. Her expression was grim as she looked Kitty up and down and Kitty could only guess at her own appearance in her out-moded clothes.

Adrian said; "Supper is ready. Mother has baked you something special. We guessed you'd be hungry after your long journey." His words and tone were conciliatory.

"I'm not hungry," she said. "I'm just very tired." She was hoping he would take the hint, but as she dragged herself up the stairs she heard him say; "I'm not hungry either, Mother. I'll go up with Kitty."

Her chin sagged on her chest. God, how she was being punished for that moment's madness with Harvey.

SIX

Kitty awoke, instantly feeling unusually refreshed. Daylight streamed into the room. She was alone in the bed; the curtains had been drawn back and the blinds raised. It was nearly ten o'clock. She had slept for twelve hours. She closed her eyes when she heard footsteps on the stairs, not wanting to face her mother-in-law's interrogation, but it was Adrian. She squinted at him through moving lids then raised them fully, feeling him staring at her. He was wearing a black suit and tie. In deference to her mother? You humbug, she thought.

"How are you? If you're not too tired I wondered if you would like a ride up West to see Hyde Park."

What was his game? Why was he so obviously trying to placate her? She didn't trust him, but she nodded, anything would be preferable to a day alone with Mrs Beatty.

"Good. I'll leave you to dress, then. I'll tell Mother not to expect us back for dinner."

He was taking her out for lunch! She hurried out of bed as soon as he had gone, wondering if his mother had passed on her suspicions of Kitty's condition. Was that the reason for his concern—for asking her if she would like to go out instead of informing her?

Such thoughts didn't trouble her for long. She was still young enough to live for the present. The thought of an outing even such an uneventful one as a ride to the West End would help to make up for her homesickness.

She didn't spend long on deciding what to wear, she had so little choice. The only black skirt she possessed was the one Maggie had altered. She put aside the black satin blouse she had worn daily for the past week and which was too big. Among her mother's things was a black georgette blouse she had had made when she was younger and slimmer. It had originally been trimmed with beige lace but Maggie had replaced that with black ribbons, and black braid had replaced the cherry-coloured ribbons on Kitty's only hat. The mirror on the tallboy only reflected as far as her waist. She didn't look too outlandish she thought, except that black didn't suit her, it made her look sallow. She pinched her cheeks and bit her lips. A little colour would improve her appearance, though why should she bother about her appearance when there was only Adrian to see?

He was waiting for her in the hall below. He looked her up and down but made no comment, and Kitty felt that she had passed his scrutiny satisfactorily. Mrs Beatty showed her displeasure by slamming the scullery door.

Adrian offered her his arm and they walked the length of Milton Street in silence. They hadn't long to wait for the bus and Adrian suggested they rode on top. Yesterday's storm had done little to cool the air, in fact the humidity had increased and Kitty was grateful for the breeze created by the moving vehicle.

The conductor had returned to the lower deck, they were the only passengers on top, Adrian cleared his throat several times. She wondered if he had something stuck in his throat. He had—words he found difficult to get out.

"Your father—your sister—they were pleased to see you?"

"Of course they were, but it wasn't the happiest of occasions—"

Another slight cough. "My mother told me that you had asked for the money for your fare. You managed to get it in the end?"

It gave Kitty great satisfaction in explaining how she had raised the money. She would love to have added that her wedding ring wouldn't have taken her as far as Swindon, but one look at his face warned her that she had said enough already; she wasn't a sadist. He had gone brick red. It pained her to look at him.

"You didn't tell your family about the brooch?" he said anxiously.

So that was it. He still wanted to retain his image of a man of substance to those who didn't know him. Why? Conceit—a shallow egotism? He cared little that she should know of his true circumstances. Perhaps he needed that image, perhaps it did something to boost his morale. For the first time her contempt of him was tinged with pity. What an empty person he was.

"My mother acted as she did for the best possible reasons," he insisted. "She thought it unwise for a young girl to travel all that way unaccompanied. That doesn't mean to say I condone her attitude. I feel she should have lent you the money." He fumbled in his waistcoat pocket and produced his coin purse. "I had better reimburse you. How much did the—eh—" he hesitated over the word pawnbroker and could not bring himself to utter it.

"How much did you realize on your brooch?"

Kitty thought of the five sovereigns Maggie had given her and felt tempted to tell him to keep his money, but commonsense prevailed. He might not make such a gesture again, and she would face many expenses in the months to come. So she took the money with a murmured 'thank you' and after that their conversation petered out for want of stimulation.

It was Kitty's first sight of the East End. She had thought Stratford grim enough but it was respectable, even pleasant, compared to the approaches of the Whitechapel Road. The people shuffled, they did not walk, there was no spring to their step. The women in drab shawls and bonnets, the men in frayed suits, the bare-footed children all had one thing in common, a look of pinched insufficiency. The easy-going progress of the omnibus made her an unwilling witness of scenes of abject poverty. She saw crowded courts and foetid alleyways. The gutters were full of decomposing vegetation steaming in the August sun and half-starved dogs fought and snarled over the debris.

She was not insensitive to the misery she saw, she knew such images would be imprinted on her mind for always; but she was glad when they changed buses and the horses clip-clopped through the busy streets of the city. When they alighted at Piccadilly, it was an entirely different world.

Kitty looked about her eagerly. She had read that Piccadilly was the hub of London and therefore the hub of the British Empire. Her first impression was one of disappointment. Here was no grand piazza or square— just a convergence of streets with Eros at the centre and flower-girls sitting on the steps around. True, there was a big hotel on one corner and a music-hall on the other but they did not make up for the magnificent cathedral or palace she had seen in her imagination. When Adrian took her arm to lead her across the road she drew back in alarm, the horses and carts were so tightly packed together it amazed her that they had room to manoeuvre. "Come on," said Adrian impatiently; "I'm hungry."

He led her down a narrow cobbled street, too narrow for a hansom-cab. It was a street of restaurants, they passed many, then stopped at one with just the one window. In the window was an aspidistra in a brass urn and standing next to it a large china figure of a heron with a frog in its mouth. Kitty wasn't impressed. Just the place Adrian would bring me to, she thought. But inside were all the signs of discreet opulence. Oak-panelling, gilt cornices, pier glasses, attentive waiters.

The clientèle was predominantly male, and this relieved Kitty's mind who had had ideas of being regarded with amused disdain by *dames de mode*. Adrian was known here; the head waiter bowed and showed them to a table. Kitty was dismayed when she saw that the menu was in French but Adrian said he would order for them both.

A bowl of dun-coloured jelly was placed before Kitty. She looked at it and frowned. "It's iced consommé," Adrian hissed. "A speciality of the house. Get on with it."

She got it down somehow, it didn't compare with the calves'-foot jelly her mother used to make when they were ill, but afterwards came a dish of lamb cutlets and they were delicious, crisp on the outside, tender and juicy inside. She had thought that was the main dish and had wondered about the lack of vegetables, but it was only an entrée, and was followed by another—a tureen of plovers in thick gravy and garnished with fingers of toast. Kitty gave one look at the stick-like legs pointing up to the ceiling and hastily rose from the table, her napkin to her mouth. A kindly waiter pointed out the ladies' cloakroom. When she returned to the table, shaken and pale, Adrian, white with rage, was dissecting his second bird. "It's obvious a place like this is wasted on you," he said. "I've ordered an omelette."

But she had lost her appetite, and picked her way through the rest of the meal while Adrian devoured mutton and potatoes and green peas, raspberry pie and cream. He was expansive and good-humoured by the time the dessert was served. The food had given him a sense of bonhomie. He lit a cigar and leaned back in his chair, leering at Kitty through the haze of smoke. She saw that he was sweating, perspiration lay in beads on his forehead and upper lip. "Did you enjoy that?" he asked.

"Thank you, yes." He had been too busy eating to notice the understanding waiter whisk away her scarcely-touched plates.

"Well then, if you're ready, we'll take a stroll down Regent Street."

Regent Street! Even in faraway Cornwall Kitty had heard of Regent Street. Harvey during his college days had spent vacations with friends in London and had described for her the wide sweep of the Quadrant and Nash's imaginative architecture. Kitty didn't know enough about architecture to appreciate the unbroken crescent of tall stucco buildings, but her eyes lighted up at the display of fashions in the glittering shops. Oh to be walking here with Maggie. How they would point and ejaculate and wonder, but Adrian looked neither to the right nor to the left, and hooked on to his arm she could no nothing but keep in step.

They crossed Oxford Street, turned left into another thoroughfare and came out onto a leafy square. On three sides of the square were imposing houses, the gardens in the middle were fenced off with iron railings. Adrian pointed out one of the houses with his stick. "In that house," he said, "I was born."

Kitty waited, masking her curiosity. "Yes, I was born there—in a garret. My mother was an under-housemaid, my father a son of the family." There was a corrosive bitterness about his voice. "So I am a bastard. Does that shock you?"—and when she didn't answer, he grasped her by her arms and began to shake her. "You don't care, do you? My father could be the Duke of Westminster or a road-sweeper, it'll be all the same to you—you just don't care." He had worked himself up into such a passion that she thought he would strike her. When he did lift his arm she flinched, but he was only hailing a passing cab. He hurried her into it and got in himself, breathing heavily. He got out his handkerchief and wiped his face and his neck and hands. She cowered in a corner, feeling sick, hoping they were going all the way back to Milton Street by cab. But at Marble Arch the cab stopped and Adrian helped her out. He was in control of himself once more, though she noticed that when he paid off the cabby his hands were shaking.

All the ladies of fashion she had ever hoped to see seemed to be strolling in the park that afternoon. Others rode past in their carriages, others again on horseback riding side-saddle in habits moulded to their figures. Adrian found two vacant seats in the shade of some trees. He folded his arms and his head fell forward and he was soon asleep. Kitty couldn't sleep, there was too much to take in. She was beginning to realize that London wasn't just one city—it was many cities within a city. Here in the West End there were no signs of poverty. Coster-mongers' barrows were easily outnumbered by broughams and landaux. There were no weary old men in suits green with age nor women worn out by hard work and child-bearing, or children bowlegged by rickets. Nothing could have brought home to her the difference between the East and West Ends of London as seeing it with her own eyes.

Adrian stirred, opened his eyes and yawned. For a few minutes he watched the changing pattern of colours as the populace went by, then he said in the tone of one bestowing a favour; "I brought you here just in the nick of time. After the twelfth, the 'Glorious Twelfth' so-called, when grouse shooting starts, London will be empty. There won't be anybody of note to be seen here or in any of the other parks, and in Mayfair all the blinds will be down in the houses. The West End will seem like a wasteland."

"What about the East End? Will that also be a waste-land?"

If he detected sarcasm in her voice he ignored it. "Would you like tea?" She would, but almost imme-diately he changed his mind. "Perhaps not, it's been a long day. We'll have tea at home." And save you any further expense, thought Kitty.

On the long ride back to Stratford she thought back to Adrian's extraordinary behaviour in the square. How much could she believe of his story that he was the result of a clandestine relationship between a servant girl and a son of her employers? It was impossible to think of Mrs Beatty either as young or desirable but such things did happen; she knew that from personal experience.

A friend of her mother's had been matron of a work-house in a village not far from Falmouth. Once she and Maggie had been taken to tea there, and looking back with hindsight, she thought, as a salutary lesson. They had been given tea in Matron's parlour and the girl who waited on them had a pinched and defeated look about her. Later they had been taken on a tour of the grim-looking granite building, and at twelve years old Kitty had not understood Matron's references to her 'bad' girls. She had been more interested in the babies and wanted to know who they belonged to but Maggie had hushed her. Later, at home, she had told Kitty the babies belonged to unfortunate girls who had got into trouble, many while in service and had been sent away in disgrace. She wouldn't or couldn't enlarge when Kitty had asked what sort of trouble?

If Adrian's story were true, and something in his behaviour had her convinced it was, it accounted for many anomalies. Their petty snobbishness for one thing. Mrs Beatty's constant references to the 'riff-raff' and 'guttersnipes' of Stratford. They had always acted as if they were socially superior to their neighbours. It accounted for the way Adrian held his mother in such small esteem and her abysmal deference to him. It might also account for Adrian's unrevealed income and his enactment of a man of means.

Kitty shifted in her seat; she had a pain low down in the middle of her back. As she moved a slight fluttering in the lower part of her abdomen caused her to draw in her breath.

Adrain turned irritably. "Why are you so restless? Is anything the matter, you look quite flushed?"

"The seat is uncomfortable, that's all."

"Well, we won't be long."

She didn't care now if the journey were to take all night. She felt as if she were in a different dimension. The baby had quickened. Under cover of her handbag she pressed the palm of her hand against her abdomen. Harvey's baby was safe—Harvey's baby was alive.

SEVEN

That night Kitty dreamed she was a child again, lost and looking for her mother. She was running alongside a wide stretch of water which seemed to go on for ever, but no matter how hard she pumped her legs, she remained glued to the same spot. She was calling and crying, but no sound issued forth from her open mouth; then suddenly her mother was there beside her—younger looking, her hair fair and curly beneath her bonnet. Her soft voice cooed comfortingly. "There—there—my handsome, don't fret—you know I wouldn't let my little precious get lost."

At the moment of awakening came the realization that it was her mother who was lost, that she would never see her again. It was a moment of truth she had never fully faced up to before. She turned her face into the pillow and wept silently. Beside her Adrian breathed noisily in his sleep. He was a restless sleeper, exuding a body heat which made the high feather bed insufferable in the closed room. It was a long time before Kitty got off to sleep again; when she awakened the second time she was alone in the bed, and sunlight filtered through the blinds.

She went to the washstand and dipped her face in the cold water. There was no sound from downstairs, but outside came the clip-clop of passing horses and the cries of the chair-mender and cats'-meat man.

She pulled up the blind and looked out. The sun was white-hot on the dusty pavements. A short way up the road a knife-grinder worked at his wheel. When she heard Adrian's step on the stair she got back into bed, drawing the quilt around her bare ehoulders as he entered the room. She noticed with sinking heart that he was wearing the old smoking jacket he kept for casual wear. Obviously he was not going to the City—it was going to be like another Sunday when the hours went by as slowly as hearses.

Adrian stood at the foot of the bed eyeing her. She sensed a change of mood. His mouth was a straight line, and a tell-tale nerve jerked in his throat.

As his prolonged stare made her feel uneasy, she broke her self-imposed rule and enquired; "Have you got the day off?"

"Have I got the day off!" he mimicked. "Am I a common labourer to be given *a day off*? It suits me to stay at home today, and I want you to join us downstairs as soon as you are dressed." He flipped a letter towards her. "This came for you by the second post. It's time you were up."

As soon as Kitty recognized Maggie's writing her pulse began to race. It was only forty-eight hours since she left Falmouth—what had happened to make Maggie write so soon afterwards? She tried to calm herself by thinking that bad news usually travelled by telegram.

It was a well-filled envelope, and when she opened it she found another letter folded within that of Maggie's. She glanced through Maggie's first, skipping it quickly until she got to the words—'It's of no use me telling you not to read the enclosed—of course you will, and a lot of heartbreak it will cause you. A letter from the dead is a mixed blessing—' She caught her breath as a rush of pain went through her. The letters on the page danced before her eyes. Only then did she pick up the other letter and stared at it as if in disbelief. It bore an English penny stamp which had not been franked, and its envelope was grimy and stained. Unsteadily she put it down again and went back to Maggie's letter, reading it afresh, very slowly;—

'—I was in two minds about forwarding this on to you. I didn't want to reopen old wounds, but on the other hand I couldn't bring myself to destroy it. A seaman called at the house with it this evening. He said that Harvey had given him this to post in Southampton. According to this man he was due to sail back to Falmouth, but through indulging too freely (his own words) he found himself in Winchester Jail on a three months' sentence for being drunk and disorderly. He docked at Falmouth today and on going through his pockets, came across the letter which until then he had forgotten, or so he says. Anyway, he came straight to Laburnum Road to deliver it;—but judging from his condition he hadn't passed a single ale-house. If he expected any reward he didn't get it.

'It's of no use me telling you not to read the enclosed— of course you will, and a lot of heartbreak it will cause you. A letter from the dead is a mixed blessing. Take care of yourself and if there is anything you really need please let me know and I'll see what I can do. I must close now or I'll miss the last post.

Your loving sister,
Maggie.

P.S. Dave and I are to be married in September. We discussed it after you left yesterday.'

The pages fluttered from Kitty's fingers. She had read the postmark twice, but it barely made sense. All the time she had been reading a refrain had been running through her mind—a letter from Harvey—a letter from Harvey. It took a lot of will-power to open it. Maggie might be right. A letter from the dead could mean mixed blessings. Even the sight of Harvey's handwriting had brought ready tears welling.

But she hadn't read further than the first three lines before the tears dried on her cheeks, and the room began to whirl about her. 'My dearest little Kitten', Harvey had written. 'I hope you will receive this letter very shortly so that you will learn of my change of plan. Fate has stepped in in the shape of an old friend and put all thoughts of going off to America out of my mind—'

Was it possible that Harvey might still be alive, that he didn't perish with the *Eugenie*? She found she had crumpled the letter so tightly in her agitation that her nails were digging into the palm of her hand. When she began to read again an urge to relieve her feelings in mad shrieks of joy swept over her.—'I was on board the *Eugenie* and ready to sail when it developed engine trouble. By the time it had been put right we had missed the tide and our sailing-time put back twelve hours. I couldn't stay in my cramped quarters that long so decided to go ashore for a spell. The first person I met on the quay was this friend I have already mentioned. He had been enquiring after me for days and only learnt that morning that I was sailing on the *Eugenie*. Talk about providence! If everything had gone as planned, he would have missed me by two hours.

'His name is John Arrowsmith, you must remember me talking about him. I sometimes stayed at his London home. His father also owned a shipping line, but up in Liverpool, not Cornwall and like mine set in his ways and wouldn't consider steam-ships. I am writing this letter to you in great haste, and in the tavern where John is staying. We've spent the last hour talking, and John has plenty to talk about. He has booked a passage on a Danish three-masted barque the *Aero* bound for Australia. It is lying off Cardiff now; its next port of call is Durban. John can talk of nothing but Australia and the hunt for gold that is on. His excitement is contagious—I've already caught the fever. With gold in our pockets we shall return to England and start our own yard—building steamships, of course. That's why John wanted me to go in with him, we think alike. He poohed-poohed my idea of making a quick fortune in America. He says the days of the pioneers are over. Australia is Eldorado now.

'My darling girl, how could I resist him? Just thinking of you, of getting back to you that much sooner, and with my pockets lined with gold! Think of it, Kitten—gold.

'John reminds me of some brilliant comet who has flared across my path and caught me up by his tail. This is no fools' errand. I'm sure it was predestined—why else should the *Eugenie* have broken down? There is so much more I would like to say, but time is precious. I must get down to the shipping-agents and see whether I can trade in my ticket on the *Eugenie* for one on the *Aero*. If not, John says he'll lend me the money. I won't have time to post this myself, as John already has a cab at the door and is urging me to hurry. The *Aero* sails tomorrow. Luckily I have spotted a chap I know from Falmouth. He's at the bar and I'll give him this and ask him to post it for me. I'll write again as soon as I'm on board. Hopefully we'll be able to go ashore at Durban. *Au revoir* my little one. A kiss for each of those bewitching eyes. What wouldn't I give for a touch of your lips! Remember me in your prayers and wish me God speed.

Yours forever,
Harvey.'

By the time she read the letter a second time, Kitty's wave of joyful hysteria had subsided, and instead niggling thoughts brought unease.

If only Harvey had posted this all-important letter himself instead of trusting it to someone he might have known was unreliable. If only she had not been so quick to rush into marriage. But the biggest 'if' of all—if only Harvey having once made up his mind to go to Australia instead of America had returned to Falmouth and talked it over with her father and herself. Together they might even have persuaded her father to let them marry after all. If not they could have eloped—somehow they could have been together, she was sure of it.

Why did certain words Maggie had uttered keep coming back to her? 'What Harvey wanted was not security but adventure'. Was that what he was seeking now—the lure of gold? No, she would not allow herself to think that, it would be a betrayal of her love. All the same she wished the word John had not recurred so often in the letter.

Again she heard Adrian's tread on the stairs and she hurriedly pushed both letters under her pillow. She knew she could not disguise the fact that she was in a highly-charged emotional state, but let Adrian think what he liked. What did it matter—Harvey was alive!

She did not look up when he entered. She couldn't bear the sight of him at the moment. If it weren't for him she would be free to marry Harvey, an afterthought that the position she found herself in was of her own making brought little comfort.

"I asked you to join us downstairs," he said. "But never

80

mind we can talk just as easily up here, better perhaps, as Mrs Daly won't be able to eavesdrop." Mrs Daly was the twice-weekly cleaning woman.

Kitty looked up to see her mother-in-law was also present, like some shrivelled-up bird of ill-omen, she thought, and looked away again mistrusting the gleam in the other's full eyes.

"Are you with child?" Adrain's sharp question was so unexpected that Kitty felt the colour flood into her cheeks. "My mother says you are, and when she discovered that I had no idea of your condition she made certain suggestions that I didn't like. I've come up here to find out the truth."

Kitty took a deep breath. Partly to steady her racing heart, partly to gain time. Her only defence lay in brazening it out. Very well then, she'd take the war into the enemy's camp.

"Your mother is more experienced in matters of this kind than I am," she said pertly. It was a tactical mistake. She could tell from Adrian's expression that she could expect no mercy from him now.

"There is only one way to settle this," he snapped. "I'll send for Dr Rogers. Mother, tell Mrs Daly to go for him—"

"She's just about to scrub the scullery floor—"

"She can leave that. I'll have this thing settled today, one way or the other. Go and tell her—"

Mrs Beatty flashed Kitty a look of malicious triumph. She thought she had won. As the door closed on her, Adrian moved closer to the bed. "Is what my mother suspects true? Are you with child?"

Kitty's brief rebellion was spent, fear began to work like a canker inside her. She still had her child to think of and Harvey was thousands of miles away. She lied desperately; "I don't know. I don't understand about such things—"

She reminded Adrian of some frightened, cornered creature; desire for her overwhelmed him and his expression relaxed. He stretched out his hand to touch her hair. It had always fascinated him, and he often insisted on unpinning it for her at night. His expression hardened again when he saw how she shrank away. No dutiful wife should have such feelings against her husband.

"Tell me," he said angrily. "If you are with child, is it my child?—my mother says not."

She remained silent, looking away.

"Answer me—answer me at once."

She looked at him then putting all the misery and humiliation of the past two months into her voice. "I wish it were anybody's child but yours. Do you really think I want to have your child? You know that I have never loved you, that you have never once tried to win my love. Do you think I'd be proud of a child born of such a union as ours!"

Her outburst shook him, and seeing him at a disadvantage, Kitty flared up again. "Now leave me. If the doctor is coming I want to be ready for him."

He went without a word and Kitty jumped out of bed and bolted the door after him. She had moved so quickly that a fit of dizziness came over her and she grabbed hold of the bedrail until it had passed. She felt she could not go on much longer on this emotional see-saw, it was taking its toll. She felt better after she had sponged herself all over and put on a clean nightgown. She took some of Adrian's eau-de-cologne and sprinkled it on her hair and dabbed it on her forehead and on her throat. She brushed out her hair and replaited it.

The room reeked of stale night air and cigar fumes. She liberally sprinkled the eau-de-cologne over the bed and chairs, and opened wide the windows. Since her baby had quickened, her bouts of nausea had lessened and the smell from the brewery no longer bothered her. She re-made the bed, put Harvey's letter in her trunk, and draped a shawl around her shoulders. Not because she was cold, but out of modesty as she had no dressing-gown. Then she sat down to wait.

She knew it was midday when the brewery hooter sounded. Soon afterwards came the smart clip-clip of horses' hooves, the doctor's gig, she suspected. The shop doorbell pinged, and perspiration began to bead her upper lip. She clasped her hands together to stop them shaking. Her spirits ebbed even further when a thin elderly man was ushered into the room by Mrs Beatty.

"Is this whom you called me out for—this child?" he said truculently.

Mrs Beatty gave one of her nervous coughs. "She's not as young as all that."

"Humph." A pair of startlingly blue eyes beneath heavy black brows regarded Kitty searchingly. "There's no need for you to stay." His manner towards Mrs Beatty was very off-hand.

She bridled. "I must stay. I'm the chaperone."

"Don't be stupid, woman, I'm old enough to be this child's grandfather. Why don't you go downstairs and put the kettle on. We shall all be needing a cup of tea, later."

When the two of them were alone, the doctor brought a chair over to the bed and sat down. For a moment or two there was silence. Then he said; "I don't know what to make of you. Whatever possessed you to marry a man like Adrian Beatty?"

Kitty lifted her eyes to his, saw his mouth quirk into a smile, and quickly looked down again. He said; "Don't do that again or I might easily forget I *am* old enough to be your grandfather."

"Do what?"

"Look at me like that, you little hussy."

He made the word sound like a term of endearment. Kitty began to feel more at ease sensing that in this curious man she might find an ally. She smiled and he patted her hand.

"Did your husband tell you I had advised him never to marry, but that if he did marry on no account to have children?"

Kitty looked startled. "We didn't discuss such things."

The doctor snorted. "I'd like to kick that fool all round Stratford. Didn't he tell you he carries a hereditary disease?"

At Kitty's blank stare, the doctor shook his head. "No, I can see he didn't. No wonder he hid himself before I arrived. Do you know anything of your mother-in-law's history?" he added abruptly.

"A little."

"I've known Lottie Beatty since she was twelve years old and I was my father's apprentice. She went into service and I didn't see her again for twenty years, when she returned to Stratford, already several months pregnant. The only family she had was a younger sister in service herself. I never liked Lottie, but I could only feel pity for her then. Still, the family she worked for stood by her. They bought her the lease on this shop and they set up a trust fund for Adrian. They educated him and found him a situation, to use one of Adrian's own genteel words, in a merchant bank in the city. Not that I think he does much work—he's away sick most of the time—but it's a convenient little subterfuge, and you may be sure the bank is not out of pocket."

Kitty thought of her husband's unhealthy pallor—the many holidays he had spent in Cornwall—his bouts of lassitude, but could feel no sympathy. Knowing all this he had married her and in other circumstances she might have been bearing his child.

"What is wrong with him?"

"I won't blind you with science, let's call it a form of jaundice but very unpleasant, and in some cases fatal. Do you know who Adrian's father was?"

She shook her head. "You say *was*."

"Oh, yes, he died quite young. A good thing in my opinion before he could do any more mischief. He would have been titled and very wealthy had he lived." The blue eyes had a scornful look to them. He leant forward and tilted Kitty's chin. "You don't look the sort of person to be impressed by a title. I wonder how that unimaginative lump came to net such a pretty little shrimp like you. You don't come from these waters, do you, not with that accent. Cornwall, I should say."

"Falmouth."

"So you exchanged Falmouth for Stratford; whatever for? Don't tell me it was for love. I'm too old to believe in love."

"It was love in a way," said Kitty, determined to confess everything. "I had to find a husband in a hurry to protect my baby, and Adrian happened."

"So that's it; now I understand," and the doctor began to chuckle. "Who would believe it of you, sitting there looking so innocent—"

Kitty blushed furiously. "It's not like that at all. I'm not that sort of a girl—"

"Forgive me, my dear, I was clumsy to say that. Of course I can see you're not that sort of a girl. Now don't cry. You'd better tell me everything."

"I've only been married two months, and I'm four months pregnant. My mother-in-law already suspects, and she has told Adrian and that's why they sent for you. When they discover the truth they will throw me out." She broke down again and he waited patiently for her to recover. "I'm not saying all this just to arouse your pity. I'm not proud of myself. I just wanted to protect my child, and to save my parents from scandal."

"The father of your child—he was not another sick man, I hope."

Kitty flung up her head with such a blaze of passion in her eyes that the doctor's thoughts on love had to be revised. "He was—is—strong and tall and gentle and kind. I worship him."

"Humph—well, just get on the bed, my dear, and we'll get this examination over."

Afterwards he confirmed that the baby could be expected in the early part of January. He sat for a while on the bed beside her, drumming his fingers on his knee and humming beneath his breath.

"We'd better get them up here and tell them," he said finally. "Don't worry," and he pressed her shoulder; "Leave all the talking to me."

He went on to the landing and bellowed down the stairs. Presently mother and son came into the bedroom. Adrian looked impassive, but his mother's eyes went from Kitty to the doctor and back to Kitty as if she already suspected a conspiracy.

Dr Rogers put on an expansive smile. When he liked he could be charming, on the whole he was very well liked in Stratford and his practice was a thriving one. "I have to congratulate you," he said to Adrian. "You are indeed going to be a father."

Adrian who had expected nothing but abuse did not know how to respond. Colour came and went in his mother's face.

"How can he possibly be the father? They've only been married two months and I know she must be nearly four months—" her words petered out under the force of the doctor's look.

"Is that so? And which famous obstetrician did you study with?"

Sarcasm was lost on Mrs Beatty. "She's been suffering from morning sickness ever since coming here, and she's beginning to show for all that she tight-laces as much as she can."

"Madam, allow me to assure you that I base my assumption on a more scientific foundation. Morning sickness—tight-lacing—Mrs Gamp, woman—Mrs Gamp. If your daughter-in-law is beginning to show, as you so elegantly express it, it's because she has a very narrow pelvis. It's the fat ladies who get away without detection, not the thin ones." Kitty recalled that Maggie had said almost the same thing. Then abruptly his bantering tone changed. "For an expectant mother she hasn't got an ounce of spare flesh on her bones. If you want a healthy child," and he purposely stressed the word healthy, looking at Adrian; "you must see that your wife gets a proper diet. Plenty of milk and eggs and meat. Get her out of this stuffy hole too. Let her have all the exercise she wants and all the rest she needs. You don't want her to lose this child, I presume."

Adrian looked bemused, cowed by the doctor's manner. A situation had developed over which he had no control. When Dr Rogers said; "Come, I want a talk with you—man to man." He meekly followed him out of the room. Mrs Beatty remained; pinched-looking, full of venom, she turned accusingly on Kitty.

"You might have pulled the wool over that old fool's eyes, my girl, but you don't deceive me. It will out in good time—it will out."

EIGHT

That night Mrs Beatty made up a camp bed for Adrian in the box-room. When he came to collect his toilet things he told Kitty that Dr Rogers had advised against them sleeping together because of the possible risk that Kitty might miscarry. Kitty sent up a silent prayer of thanks and gratitude. The elderly doctor had seen deeper into her suffering than she had realized.

She had been sitting on the edge of the bed brushing her hair when Adrian came in. He collected together his shaving brush, razor and strop and put them in a bag. Then with an abruptness that startled her he crossed the room and grasped a rope of her hair. He stared at it morosely for a second or two then coiled it about her throat.

"What a slender little neck. One pull on this and it

would snap. How would you like to be strangled with your own hair?" The look on his face was ghastly. Kitty tried to pull his hands away. "Stop it, you're hurting me."

"I wish I had the courage to strangle you, that would get you out of my system, wouldn't it?" To her embarrassment he suddenly fell on his knees and sobbed loudly. Then he quietened down, took hold of her hair again, but gently this time, burying his face in it. "You don't love me—you'll never love me, but it doesn't matter now, you are carrying my child. Give me a son, a healthy son, and nothing will be too good for you—nothing!"

She couldn't bear to look at him drooling in that fashion at her feet. She wished she could feel pity, because he looked so pitiful, but instead, the revulsion she had for him increased. He must have sensed this. He went very still then rose unsteadily to his feet. He picked up his shaving tackle and hair brushes and left the room without looking at her again. Wearily, she closed and bolted the door after him.

From the time of Dr Roger's visit, life such as it was began to improve. Meals became plentiful and varied and her movements were not questioned. Adrian made no further attempt at conciliation; her mother-in-law however expressed her feelings adequately in brooding looks and silent antipathy.

The heat wave went on and Kitty wilted under the weight of her mourning clothes. She thought wistfully of her white muslin dress and the idea came to her that it might be possible to have it dyed. She had not yet redeemed her brooch from the pawnbroker, and there was a certain package she wanted to post to Maggie. She decided on all three errands one afternoon.

She went to the post office first and bought a registered-letter, not trusting Harvey's ring or letter to the ordinary post. She had made up her mind to send them to Maggie for safe keeping after finding her trunk disturbed and guessed Mrs Beatty had been rummaging around.

As she entered the pawnbroker's, later, the door was pulled from her hand and out flounced a young woman shouting abuse over her shoulder. They all but collided.

"Oops—sorry, ducks," the woman smiled in a friendly manner. She had an abundance of red hair which was escaping untidily from beneath a floppy silk hat. Her red and white striped jacket was fastened with jet buttons and matching ear-rings dangled almost to her shoulders. Goldy-brown eyes stared boldly at Kitty and affronted, Kitty drew her mantle more closely around her.

When she came out of the pawnshop she was dismayed to find the woman still there, lolling against the window, idly picking her teeth.

"Wouldn't he take it then?" jerking with her thumb towards the shop.

"I don't follow you."

"Come off it, luv, don't play the high and mighty with me. You went in with a parcel, and you came out with the same parcel. No sale, eh?"

With a disdainful shrug Kitty turned to walk away when a sudden attack of nausea came over her and she felt violently sick. The taste of the greasy chop Mrs Beatty had given her for dinner rose up in her throat and a fit of giddiness made her grab at the door handle for support. The face of the red-headed woman loomed into focus; "God, you look awful—here, let me help—"

"I feel sick. I'm going to be sick," Kitty moaned.

"Hang on to me—I only live round the corner—"

A nightmarish few minutes followed with Kitty fighting down wave after wave of sickness determined not to vomit in public. She was only dimly aware of being hoisted along a street of terraced cottages, through a door, a room, another door, a backyard—and blessed relief—a W.C. Voices drifted through the partition.

"Who is she, Vi? Friend of yourn?"

"No—I only just met her at Max's. I thought she looked seedy so I hung around. Good thing I did. Put the kettle on, Ma, she'll want a cup of tea."

Then came a hazy recollection of a small cluttered room, a chair with a cushion at her back, her blouse being undone and her stays loosened. "Poor kiddo, she's in the family way. I thought as much."

Kitty opened her eyes and saw concern on the face of the red-headed woman. She smiled wanly and the other responded with a wide grin revealing strong white teeth, even but slightly protruding. She was not handsome, her features were too coarse, but there was a brazen charm about her and she had a good figure.

Standing by her was a tiny little woman in a cross-over overall. A hump between her shoulders thrust her head forward, giving her the questing look of a bright-eyed little bird. "How you feel now, dearie?" she said.

"Oh, much better thank you," Kitty replied, struggling to sit upright. She was merely being polite. She didn't feel much better at all. The room was so small and there was a fire in the grate. Vi soon realized this.

"It's like a bloody oven in here," she said. "Open the door, Ma."

The door opened straight on to the street. A woman shuffling past in a man's cap, looked in, nodded, and went on.

"I had to make the fire up to get me ironing done." The little woman complained. "You didn't leave me any pennies for the gas." Quick as lightning she had whipped the ironing blanket off the table and spread a white cloth instead. Cups and saucers appeared, a tea-pot, milk, sugar and a seed cake. Soon they were sitting round talking like old friends. Kitty had not felt so much at home since leaving Falmouth.

She learnt that Vi was a barmaid working at the Silver Cascade music-hall in the Broadway, and that Ma

Watling was not her mother as she has at first supposed, but her landlady and also worked at the Silver Cascade as a part-time wardrobe mistress and seamstress. In turn Kitty told them about Cornwall and Maggie and Dave and her father. She didn't mention Harvey and saw no reason to tell them about Adrian though both had looked at her wedding ring. It was only when Vi asked why she was wearing black on such a hot day that she could even bring herself to talk about her recent bereavement. She was to learn in the following months that Vi Spencer had a way of firing questions like arrows, and they invariably hit their mark.

"What happened to my parcel?"

"It's safe, why?"

"It's my white muslin dress; I want to get it dyed black. I was looking for a dyers and cleaners. Do you know of one?"

When Vi smiled her white teeth braided her lower lip like a rim. In a district where most of the women over thirty had few teeth remaining, hers were outstanding. By contrast, Ma Watling could only display three broken blackened teeth, but then she was in her sixties. "You needn't look any further than thirty-three Nelson Street, duckie," she said. "I do all the dying for the Cascade dancers. I'm good at it, ain't I, Vi? Let's see your dress."

She examined it with a professional eye. "I don't see any problem wiv' that. I'll go and look me dye-bags over. I think I've got some already."

"You hard up, kid?"

From the tiny lean-to kitchen they could hear Ma Watling rummaging through a drawer. Nervously Kitty twisted the wedding-ring on her thin finger, it was much looser than when she first wore it. "Can't you tell by my clothes? Aren't you curious about me being in a pawn-broker's?"

"That ain't any of my business and you can always tell

me when you want. As for your clothes, they were good once, but they weren't made for you. Is your husband outer work? It's nothing to be ashamed of, half this street is on short time, we're always popping in and outer Max's—"

"I went to redeem something, and, yes, my husband is in work." Kitty looked straight at Vi. "I'd rather not talk about him."

The other's strange tawny-coloured eyes looked very understanding. "All right, luv—if you don't, you don't. Milton Street? I know a cove from Milton Street—don't know his name—we call him the Squire or Broadway. He looks as if he owns half the place and is considering buying the other half. Large fishy eyes—his mother runs a little corner draper's. You wouldn't know him, I suppose?"

"Yes, I know him," said Kitty dully. "I'm married to him."

"An' Ma always telling me I open my mouth too wide and put my boot in it. Sorry ducks." But Vi didn't look sorry or even embarrassed, more curious. She was on the point of firing another question, then thought better of it and to fill up the silence which followed, Kitty asked; "How is it you know my husband?"

"I can't say I know him. I've just seen him at the Silver Cascade. He used to come in for a drink and to watch the dancing girls. Hasn't been lately."

Ma came in with a fresh pot of tea and a small black bottle. "I've found the dye. I'll do your dress tomorrow; it should 'ave dried by the day after—"

"You must let me pay you."

"Rubbish," said Vi. She reached down a different kind of black bottle from the top shelf of the dresser. "A little drop of something in your tea to bring the roses back to your cheeks? No? Then you won't mind if Ma and I do." She poured a generous dose of whisky in their cups. "It's good for Ma's heart, an' I take it to keep me spirits up. Down the hatch!"

"Tell me about the Silver Cascade." Kitty wondered what appeal it had held for Adrian. The dancing girls? He'll be back there soon, she thought cynically.

"There ain't much to tell, really. It was only built a couple of years ago on the site where the old Empire used to be that got burnt down. I preferred the old Empire, that was more homely. But the Silver Cascade ain't a bad little crib, and the Guv'nor pays well—"

"She don't do at all bad," said Ma, breaking in. "Better money than what she got at the Empire." She expounded on the Cascade. It was owned by a wealthy American, or at least someone who had spent many years there, a Bruno Chalk. ("Ain't nobody going to convince me that's his real name"). He also owned a twin establishment in the West End too grand to go by the title of music-hall and known as the Golden Cascade. ("On account of the sovereigns and half-sovereigns what rattle into the tills there. Down here its only sixpences and threepenny bits").

"Ma, shut up," said Vi laughing. "Can't you see Kitty don't even know what a music-hall is."

That was true. Kitty had heard of them, but her strict chapel upbringing had precluded any visit to a theatre or similar establishment. She wondered what Maggie would make of Vi. What would she think of Kitty's swift friendship with a barmaid? Did it matter? Maggie was miles away and Kitty needed friends badly, and, in the weeks that followed, the small, overcrowded, untidy, ever-welcoming cottage in Nelson Street became very dear to her. It was the nearest she had now to a home and like a home it became her bolt-hole.

Her first reaction to learning that Vi's hair was not natural but that it was hennaed to obtain its vivid tints, was not one of shock as it would have been a year ago, but one

94

of keen interest to see how it was done. She had matured sufficiently to realize that faults such as malice, meanness and churlishness could cause more harm than a little bit of henna or a dab of rouge. Now she became inured to seeing Vi sitting with her head plastered in green paste, but could never get used to the manner in which she cleaned her teeth—with a bar of Hudson's soap. "My ole man cleaned his with soot," she said when Kitty first exclaimed over it. "But I never took to that myself. Soap suits me a treat, and I bet you never saw whiter teeth than mine," and there she was correct.

Vi knew a woman who kept a secondhand clothes shop and from her got Kitty a crêpe dress and matching jacket trimmed with jet beads. She said the two had cost five shillings.

"You didn't get these for five shillings. They've hardly been worn—they must be worth much more."

"Vi knows how to strike a hard bargain, she do," chortled Ma Watling. "She's bin buying clothes off Mrs Tozer for years, she don't owe her nothing." The dress was tight but the little seamstress made short work of letting out the seams. She worked deftly either with the machine or by hand. She had dyed the white muslin to perfection.

"Where does this Mrs Tozer get hold of such things?"

"Ladies' maids mostly. They sell the things their mistresses pass on to them. Mrs Tozer's got a lot of contacts up West. Look what else I brought back from Angel Lane." Vi held up a small straw bag dripping water. "Lovely cockles, fresh today from Southend. Get your sewing machine off the table, Ma, so we can have tea. If you ain't tasted cockles before, Kitty, you're in for a treat."

Vi liberally annointed Kitty's plate with vinegar and pepper. Ma cut generous slices from a cottage loaf still warm from the baker's. Kitty indulged herself rather too well.

She paid for it that night. She dreamt she saw Harvey drowning. She was rowing one of her father's skiffs, but every time she got within reach of him a huge breaker came and bore him further away. The worst part of all was that he made no attempt to save himself but lay on the water as if already dead. Then came a final wave curling over in a mountain of water and tossed Harvey away as if he were a piece of flotsam, and as he sank out of sight she let out a shrill scream of anguish.

She awoke suddenly and realized she had screamed in reality for Adrian was beside her, shaking her. His flickering candle cast a shadow on the ceiling.

"What is the matter. Are you in pain?"

"No—no—I'm all right. I had a dream, a bad dream. I expect I ate something that disagreed aith me—"

He was bending over her so closely she could feel his breath on her face. "Would you like me to stay with you?"

It was too dark to see the look on his face but there was expectancy in his voice. She felt a sickness in the pit of her stomach and her heart pounded. She turned her head on the pillow.

"Please leave me. I don't feel very well."

"You were well enough to go round to Nelson Street again today." He didn't approve of her new friends but surprisingly had not forbidden her to visit them, perhaps not risking another confrontation with Dr Rogers. "What did you have for tea?"

"Some new bread—"

"Little fool." She felt his hand on her face; he stroked her cheek then her throat. He was tugging at the buttons on her nightgown when she said weakly; "I think I'm going to be sick."

He left her without saying any more, and she didn't bother to bolt the door after him, knowing he wouldn't be back, but there was no more sleep that night. She lay thinking of Harvey. She regretted now her hasty decision to send his letter to Maggie—that alone in the long hours like this would have been of some comfort.

Maggie had now married and was living in a cottage near the harbour. The wedding had been very quiet, there had been no reception and no photographs. "Why waste money we can't afford?" she had written, not out of bitterness but from plain commonsense, but Kitty sensed a trace of bitterness in the words which followed. "I was married in the same dress I wore to Mother's funeral. I hope it doesn't mean bad luck."

Sometimes during those late summer days Kitty was overcome with such dejection that she would curl up like a child and weep bitterly, even when she was at Nelson Street with Vi's good company and Ma Watling's motherly concern. She missed Maggie, she missed her mother, but she ached for Harvey. That golden day in early spring when they had stood in the ruins of Tregorra church and vowed eternal love seemed so far away as to be on another plane of life. Then in the midst of her misery her baby would kick, and that always brought consolation. Harvey was alive—his child was alive—one day everything would come right for them. If she could but hang on to that thought she could face anything.

One fine day in October Vi took her for a tram ride to Wanstead Flats. They rode through Leytonstone, an expanding suburb which still retained much of its rural past, with farmland interspersed by solitary weather-boarded cottages, then rows of newly built red-brick villas with neat gardens. When they alighted at the flats Kitty could imagine herself deep in the country.

Epping Forest started here. Vi led the way across rough grass to a pond where mallard and moorhens dipped and paddled among the reeds. The ground was dry enough to sit on, and they lounged, removing their hats. The trees around them made shifting patterns of brown and orange and yellow as the wind ruffled the leaves. Except for a man and a boy flying a kite some distance away there was nobody in sight.

Vi took a bar of nougat out of her pocket and breaking off a piece offered it to Kitty. "I hope nuts don't give you heartburn. I love nougat." She pronounced it 'nugget', then in an unusually reminiscent mood went on to speak of her childhood.

She had been the eldest of eleven children and her father, a docker, had never been certain of regular employment. As soon as they were twelve she and her brothers and sisters had left school to go out to work to swell the family income. Two of her sisters had been apprenticed to tailors, working from half-past eight in the morning until ten at night for a shilling a day. Another was on piece-work at a local match factory turning out match-boxes at twopence-ha'penny a gross. At twenty-two she had developed varicose veins from standing from six-thirty until six in summer, and eight until six in winter. Her mother, before she died, had taken in 'home' work, mostly finishing trousers. On good days she could make one-and-tuppence, but out of that had to find her own thread and gimp and soap.

"Our house wasn't a home, it was a sweat-shop," said Vi viciously, screwing up the nougat paper and aiming it at one of the ducks. "I left there when I was fifteen. I wanted to go on the stage but I hadn't the looks or the talent. Lucky for me I met Ma Watling. She was wardrobe mistress at the old Empire and took me on as a helper. I was there ten years, then when the Silver Cascade was built I was offered a job in the bar. I jumped at it." She gave one of her coarse laughs. "That's when my hair turned from light brown to red. Well, I had to have a bit of style didn't I! I know there's some what thinks I'm no better than I should be, but let 'em, I say. I belong to meself and I owe no man nothing. I work hard and I save hard. D'you know what I'm saving for?"

"Tell me."

"A nice little tea-shop, somewhere in a place like this or Woodford where I can look outer the window and see trees and grass instead of rows and rows of houses. Where I can sit behind me own counter and wear a black silk blouse and get to know all me regular customers, and have my waitresses decked out in fancy aprons and streamers—"

Kitty smiled. "What does Ma Watling think?"

"She'd come with me, of course. She'd be a good help in the kitchen. Well anyway, I can dream, can't I? It don't cost anything to dream."

Vi lowered herself down until she was lying flat on her back, her arms above her head staring dreamily at the sky.

"What about marriage, Vi? Have you ever been in love?"

"Marriage—you can keep marriage, nothing but hard work and brats. My mother was bloated with dropsy by the time she was fifty, all due to childbearing. Love—that's a different kettle of fish. Yes, I've been in love—once, but it didn't last long, not on his side. I wouldn't want to repeat it. What about you, ducky? Have *you* ever been in love?"

Kitty reddened. It was pointless making out she loved her husband, Vi knew differently. A sudden longing to talk about Harvey came over her, and Vi listened without interrupting, her tawny eyes on Kitty's face all the time.

"So that's the way of things," she commented drily, when Kitty stopped speaking. "I wondered what on earth possessed you to marry Adrian Beatty—he ain't your type. Harvey—Harvey Stephens—nice name. D'you think you'll get away with it?"

"What d'you mean?"

"Passing off your lover's child as your husband's. Not but what it hasn't been done before—"

99

"*Harvey* is my husband."

"Kitty, use your noodle! Who's going to be taken in by a bit of whim-wham like that. I'm surprised your precious Harvey let you believe—"

"I won't have a word said against Harvey!"

"All right—all right—*fainits*—I don't wanter quarrel with you, but remember dearie, when the time comes and there should be trouble in Milton Street, there'll always be a place for you and your baby with Ma and me."

Kitty's rush of anger faded, tears welled instead. "Why should you be so king to me? You don't owe me anything."

Vi rose to her feet, brushed the loose grass from her skirt, replaced her hat and speared it into place with hat-pins. "I could say because you remind me of a young sister who died when she was about your age, and that wouldn't be completely untrue. She had great dark eyes like yourn. But the real reason is I've seen too many girls caught in the same trap as you and ending up on the streets because they had no money and nowhere to turn to. It ain't going to happen to you—not if Vi Spencer can prevent it. You could do worse than come to the Cascade to work. I could always put in a word for you."

NINE

From the outside the Silver Cascade did not look all that imposing, thought Kitty, as she surveyed the red brickwork and neo-Gothic interstices, but, inside, she got quite a different impression. Vi took her straight to the bar with its polished mahogany counter and brass beertaps. "What do you think of this? Grand, eh? Knocks the old Empire into a cocked hat."

"I feel like an intruder," whispered Kitty back, overawed by the sight of rows of empty seats and silent proscenium. Vi had wanted to show her where she worked ever since their visit to Wanstead.

"Don't be so daft," said Vi impatiently. "What harm are we doing? Anyway, the place don't open until seven o'clock; we're the only two here."

The stage was draped with blue velvet decorated with

101

tinsel bows, too flashy for Kitty, but she wouldn't hurt Vi's feelings by saying so who thought everything perfect. The ceiling was midnight blue with imitation stars. Blue and silver were the predominating colours; even the plaster scroll-work of the cornices was picked out with silver. It was gaudy but bright and Kitty could understand Vi's admiration.

"But you should just see the Golden Cascade," said Vi in that tone of voice usually reserved for worshippers at a shrine. "I went up there to help out once when one of their barmaids was taken ill sudden. Cor'—red plush and gilt and flowers everywhere. Makes this place look anaemic."

"Are you in charge here?"

"Not what you call in charge, exactly, though I do nine-tenths of the work. I assist Flo Lang, but she's getting past it, poor ole soul. It's the standing—her legs swell something awful. When she do go I expect I'll be in charge. I could put in a word for you then—" and she gave Kitty a nudge.

"You surely don't think—" Kitty was saying when a door at the side of the stage opened and a slight, dapper, middle-aged man came through. Kitty heard Vi's—"Oh, my gawd!", then aloud; "Good morning, Mr Chalk, I didn't expect to find you here. I was just showing a friend around. I hope you don't mind." Vi could when she liked put a a 'refeened' accent. It didn't sound a bit like the Vi Kitty knew at all.

The newcomer stared at Kitty, and she felt herself go hot. She was glad her figure was hidden by her mother's old mantle. She was well-advanced in pregnancy now.

"Won't you introduce me to your friend?"

Vi did so and Kitty felt her hand taken by a hand small and white enough to belong to a woman. She looked into a pair of unusual eyes, dark with heavy white lids. His hair was dark too, parted in the middle and sleeked down with macassar oil. He wore a black cutaway coat over grey-striped trousers, and light grey spats partially covered black patent-leather shoes. He wore a gold watch chain from which dangled a set of seals and a sovereign set in intricate gold filigree. She knew that both her father and Harvey would have taken a dislike to him on sight. There was something of the dandy about him, something almost feminine in his demeanour, yet he gave the impression of a shrewd business man.

"I have been going through the books the manager left for me. But I must go on my way now." Why does he feel he has to explain his presence, Kitty wondered. He is the boss. Then she realized he was still clasping her hand and that Vi was giving her a sly look.

She swiftly withdrew her hand and Bruno Chalk smiled. "Good morning ladies, I hope we shall meet again." He put on his hat and walked away with swift light steps.

"The old masher," sniggered Vi. "Didn't he give you the eye!"

"Vi—that's vulgar—"

"Keep your hair on, duckie, I meant it as a compliment. You should see the girls what work at the Golden Cascade. He picks 'em himself. They've all got something about them, I don't know what it is. You've got it. It's a look—a tone of voice—a touch of class. Some of the girls here 'ud give their eye-teeth to get transferred to the Golden Cascade. He comes along every now and then to give them a look over, but if they're anything like me they stand as much chance as a dish of okey-pokey in 'Ell." She let out a gusty sigh. "Come on girl, I'm famished, and Ma's got a dish of tripe and onions keeping hot in the oven."

It was to be some time before Kitty got a chance to visit the little house in Nelson Street again. Adrian went down with one of his bad spells, and spent most of the day sitting hunched over the fire, morose and silent.

There was no point in antagonizing him, so she stayed at home working on her baby's layette, trying not to let her thoughts dwell too longingly on Ma Watling's generous fires and Vi's fount of good humour.

St. Luke's Little Summer had given way to the murky days of early November. Days when yellow fog pressed against the windowpanes. It was Kitty's first experience of a London fog, and while it hung about she had no wish to go out. Even going as far as the post-office was enough for her. When she undressed that night she found that her cotton petticoat was black up to her knees. She guessed her grey flannel petticoat was just as dirty but that didn't show. There was no question of washing it until the spring.

One morning when a fine drizzle had washed away the remains of the fog Kitty decided she couldn't stay away from Nelson Street any longer, but as she came downstairs in her outdoor clothes, Mrs Beatty heard her, and barred the way, her arms crossed in front of her narrow chest.

"And where do you think you're off to?"

"I'm going out. I've been cooped up too long."

"We've all been cooped up as you put it. Have you no thought for your husband?"

"I haven't seen him this morning. I presumed he'd gone to work.

Her mother-in-law's face took on a pinched, beaky look. "*Work—work*—he doesn't work. He *attends* his place of business when he is well enough. But what do you care? You haven't even enquired after him. He's not well enough even to leave his bed this morning."

"I'm sorry, I didn't know. Have you sent for the doctor?"

Mrs Beatty's thin lips turned up in a sneer. "And a fat lot of good that would do. We all know who's side he's on, don't we!" She couldn't keep up the sarcasm. There was genuine concern in her expression. "If you'd only show some feeling for him."

"I've said I'm sorry—what else do you expect of me?" I can't go to his room—I can't, thought Kitty in desperation. She took refuge in bluster. "It isn't as if you would let me help in the house or serve in the shop or do the cooking. You try to make me feel as much in the way as possible, then complain if I go out—"

"It isn't the going out I mind. It's the company you keep. Low-down barmaids—mixing with them no better than they should be—"

Colour ran up into Kitty's cheeks, her eyes widened with anger. "I don't suppose Adrian has told you that he was glad enough of such company before he married me. Not that I blame him—anything's better than this smelly little hole—"

She had never shouted at her mother-in-law before, never lost her temper. She had a glimpse of a startled face, angry bulging eyes, before she brushed past and slammed the door behind her. She stood on the doorstep, grasping the lintel of the door until the ground stopped rocking. Scenes like that wouldn't do her any good—wouldn't do her baby any good either. She shivered as the damp air struck through her thin clothing. Her mantle was unlined and had been made for summer wear. But oh! it was so good to be out of that place. She walked on, her head bent against the rain, tears very near. "Harvey—dear Harvey," she repeated his name silently like a plea for mercy.

Every day now she watched for the post hoping desperately for an enclosure from Maggie bearing a Durban postmark. Surely Harvey had reached South Africa by now? She had no idea how long a letter would take to come from there, and had no one to ask.

Halfway along Nelson Street she saw a stumpy figure

105

pushing an old baby-carriage, the handle of which just reached her chin. It was Ma Watling.

With a little effort Kitty caught up with her. The carriage held a bundle tied up in a sheet.

"Hello dearie, we ain't seen much of you lately." Ma greeted her with her usual gummy smile. "Not bin well, ain't you?"

"It's been too foggy to come out."

"Fog! Call that fog. Wait 'til we get a real pea-souper. I'd rather 'ave fog than this 'ere drizzle. Gets right through to me hump an' gives me gippo. What d'you think of me carriage? It's seen better days but it's alright for collecting the mending from the Cascade."

The sight of the baby-carriage jogged Kitty's memory. "I've been meaning to ask Vi if she knows anyone with a secondhand carriage or bassinette. She seems to know where to get most things. I've got all the clothes ready now, but nothing to put baby in."

"What's the point of spending out good money? What's wrong wiv a drawer to put the baby in? Makes a cosy little crib; we didn't use nothing else in my fambley. They only needed a knife-drawer for me," Ma added with a titter.

Vi was toasting muffins, her hair swathed in a towel, her blouse unfastened, her skirt pulled up to her knees so that she got the full force of the fire.

"You look like an Eastern houri," said Kitty.

Vi turned the muffin and spiked it on the other side. "So you know what an Eastern houri looks like, do you? More'n I do." She grinned over her shoulder. "Nice to see you again, girl." The last muffin toasted, she placed it with the others in a covered dish in the fireplace while she helped Ma to clear the table of sewing and mending and linen still to be ironed. "Come on, draw up a chair. There's enough for all."

The muffins were dripping with butter. Ma made tea the colour of tannin. Kitty ate and drank with relish, revelling in convivial company once more.

By the end of the meal Vi's hair was dry and redder than ever. She shook it out so that the others could admire it. "One o' these days its gorner turn green," Ma warned.

Vi took up a hair-pin and began to pick her teeth.

"Bruno Chalk came back to the Silver Cascade the other night," she said, looking at Kitty. "He sat at the bar some time talking to me. I bet you don't know who we were talking about?"

"I don't suppose it was me," said Kitty, knowing from Vi's look that it was.

"He just wanted to know where you come from and who you was married to. He's noticed your ring. Anyway, to cut a long story short, he's invited us both up to the Golden Cascade one afternoon as his guests. What do you make of that!"

"No."

"What d'you mean, no? I thought you'd be bowled over."

"Vi—how could you? In my condition!"

"Don't be so bloomin' priggish. Who's going to notice anyway, in that tent you wear. Anyway, Bruno Chalk is old enough to be your father. Come on, be a sport. Let's go next week, on my day off."

"It's impossible. I can't."

There was an ominous glint in Vi's tawny eyes. Seeing it Ma scuttled off to the safe harbour of her kitchen.

"Kitty, do this for my sake. It may be my one chance to better myself. The Guv'nor has never noticed me before—I was just one of the fittings as far as he was concerned. If I could just get to the Golden Cascade as a dresser—help in the bar—anything, it could make all the difference. I'm not that young, I'm nearly thirty, what future is for me even at the Silver Cascade? What'll happen to me eventually? Barmaid at some seedy little back street ale-house? Up West I could make contacts—"

"What about your dream of having your own tea-shop?"

"And that's all it is, a dream—you know that. I'll never get my tea-shop while I'm stuck in Stratford—I've got to get out. Oh Kitty, please—"

Kitty hesitated. "If it means that much to you, Vi, but—I can't understand why Mr Chalk wants to see me. He must know I'll never be able to work for him. I'll have my baby to look after, and when Harvey comes—"

Vi made an impatient gesture. "You mean *if* he ever comes. Face the facts, Kitty—you would have heard by now. No, alright, I won't say anymore about your precious Harvey. So you will come? Next week, the thirteenth? Pity about the date, but that's my day off. You're not superstitious?"

"No."

"I am. Still—keep our fingers crossed, eh?"

Kitty had not been entirely truthful when she said she wasn't superstitious, she had enough Celt blood in her to be a little. She always bowed to the new moon and said good morning to a chimney-sweep and wished on the tail of a piebald horse. Her mother would never seat thirteen to a table and one Christmas when Kitty was long past the toddler stage, she had found herself back in her high-chair to avoid that calamity. Still, she never worried about the thirteenth unless it fell on a Friday; then she avoided wearing green or bringing may blossom into the house. But when this particular thirteenth came round, Adrian felt so much better he decided he would go to his office, and Kitty felt the old superstition had been confounded.

The fog was back, creeping up from the nearby marshes in a yellow sulphurous haze which thickened as it collected the grime and the smoke from the factory chimneys. By nightfall it could become the pea-souper she had heard so much about. She hoped they'd be back from the West End by then.

She met Vi by arrangement at the tram-stop. Vi had certainly put herself out to make an impression. She was wearing her jet ear-rings and brooch to match, and the little red and black striped jacket which suited her, but over that was a feathered cape of dubious origin. Her crowning glory was a black velour hat with a curved brim, its only decoration a curled white feather standing up in the front like a huge question mark. Kitty managed to hide her dismay; Vi made no attempt to. She eyed Kitty up and down and said; "My God girl, you look like something out of a penny dreadful."

In fact Kitty had been rather pleased with her appearance and had studied herself carefully in the glass before leaving Milton Street. In the past week Vi had made another visit to Mrs Tozer (which accounts for that awful cape and hat, thought Kitty) purposely to find something warm in place of the alpaca mantle in which Kitty had shivered for so long. She had come back with a grey worsted cloak with hood attached and lined with red silk. It had seen better days, but it was warm and covered Kitty from head to feet.

Though her body was now swollen her face had become very thin. She had taken to dressing her hair low, bringing it down over her cheeks to give the appearance of width. She thought the hood had a softening effect, and the red lining was flattering, complementing the redness of her lips and giving an extra glow to her dark eyes. Vi thought otherwise. "I only got you that to wear locally. It's not suitable for the West End—you look as if you've come outer some charity school." She stopped grumbling as their tram approached. "I hope there's room inside. I don't fancy sitting upstairs in this weather." There was room inside. They sat squashed together on the wooden seat facing the other passengers.

Some were strap-hanging rather than face the elements outside. At Aldgate they changed into an omnibus and Vi's spirits revived. She took pleasure in pointing out different landmarks as they came to them. Kitty was interested but couldn't help wishing that Vi would lower her voice. Others besides herself were getting a conducted tour of London.

"That there is Aldgate Pump which means we're in the City proper now. This is Cheapside—I don't know why it's called that—this is where the money rolls. We just passed Leadenhall Market—you can't see it from here; I'll take you one day. This is Holborn Viaduct; the old Fleet River's down there, so one of me customers told me. Look at them insurance offices—grand enough to be a castle. Look—look—we're just passing the Holborn Empire! They get all the top-liners there. Mind you, we ain't doing so bad at the Silver Cascade. We've got Marie Lloyd coming next week. She's only eighteen, but they say she's got a future. This is Oxford Circus, we turn off here into Regent Street."

Kitty remembered Regent Street. She had walked it with Adrain. "Not far now to Trafalgar Square," went on Vi relentlessly, "That's where we get off."

A man siting opposite leaned forward to address them. "You ain't thinking of going to Trafalgar Square, are you, lady?"

"What's that to do with you?"

"Just a warning that's all. The unemployed are holding a protest rally there today. It could turn nasty."

Vi grinned good-naturedly. "The unemployed ain't got nothing to fear from me, mate. Me own father belonged to them long enough. I might even join in their protest."

"I'm only trying to tell you it's no place for two women on their own."

Kitty pulled at Vi's arm. "Perhaps we shouldn't go."

"Rubbish. I wanted to show you Trafalgar Square. Didn't you say how disappointed you was with Piccadilly Circus, about being the hub of London and nothing to show for it? Well, you won't be disappointed in Trafalgar Square, it's got everything. Nelson's Column, fountains, great broad pavements, pigeons—besides it ain't all that far from the Golden Cascade."

"Don't say I didn't warn you," said the man, standing up to ring the bell as the bus passed Haymarket. The omnibus stopped again at the east side of Trafalgar Square for the horses to have one of their customary two minutes' rests. "We may as well get out here," said Vi, helping Kitty to her feet.

Trafalgar Square was black with people, mostly men in working clothes. There was no question of the girls seeing the fountains or walking the broad pavements or admiring Nelson's Column. Kitty was filled with apprehension and even Vi went quiet.

Men converged in orderly fashion to their focal point. They came from Villiers Street, the Strand, Charing Cross Road and Pall Mall. Some carried banners, some were singing; all looked pathetically thin and ill-clad.

"Let's get outer here," said Vi; "there's going to be trouble. See them mounted police? They ain't here for show."

The mounted police closed ranks and began to surge forward; just like rounding up sheep, thought Kitty. She was no longer frightened of the mass of unemployed, her fears were all for them. Those she could see plainly looked as if they hadn't had a decent meal in weeks. Suddenly all was confusion, men were running; there was panic—screams—curses—the whinnying of horses. The police had charged.

"Come on," said Vi, clutching her arm. "We'll dodge down here." But as they attempted to cross a side-street they were caught up in a body of fleeing men. Kitty felt

Vi's arm pulled away. She screamed her name aloud but Vi was taken further away from her. The white plume on her hat seemed like a pathetic signal of surrender.

Kitty tried to push against the rioters, but they were bearing her away in another direction. She lost her footing and would have fallen but for a ready arm. She was picked up like a sack of potatoes and put up against a lamp-post for support.

"What the 'ell do you think you're doing 'ere in your condition?" Her rescuer was roughly spoken, but not unkind. He looked concerned. "You stay 'ere till this lot's gone past. Hang on to the lamp-post in case you're swep' away again."

Kitty shut her eyes against the sight of charging police, of truncheons too freely used and rearing horses with flaying hooves. Bodies lay inert, blood streaming from wounds. She found herself praying; praying was better than screaming, then a sudden, sharp pain in her side nearly doubled her in two.

She clung to the lamp-post like a drunken woman, her cheek pressed against the cool iron, her tears flowing, and it was here that Bruno Chalk found her.

"Mrs Beatty! You are ill."

"No—no—I'm quite all right." She turned her head so that he would not see her face when another pain racked her.

"As soon as I heard there was rioting in Trafalgar Square I came in search of you. I was worried about you—about you both, with all this riff-raff—"

"They are not riff-raff," she said, gasping on another pain. "They are only men grown desperate because they can't find work—"

She heard Bruno laugh. She still would not look at him. "So—little Mrs Beatty is a radical. Good for you, I've always admired a rebel—in a good cause. Come, you need help. Take my arm, my carriage is near."

"But Vi—I lost Vi."

"And I found her. She is in the carriage waiting for you."

Vi had not come through the skirmish unscathed. Her plume was missing and her feathered cape in tatters, but her light eyes blazed with triumph. Mr Chalk had come to her rescue personally, and she was now queening it in his carriage. Revolutions have started for less! She alighted when she saw Kitty.

"Duckie, you look *awful*. What's the matter?"

"My pains have started," muttered Kitty in an urgent whisper.

"Oh my God! Not today—not on the thirteenth. You can't have a baby on the thirteenth."

"I'll have it here on the street if I don't get home soon."

Whether Bruno Chalk had overheard or whether he had summed up the situation already, he acted quickly and with discretion. He helped Kitty into the carriage and gave instructions to the coachman to drive to Stratford without delay. With great aplomb Vi waved goodbye, but Kitty didn't even glance back at her benefactor. She only wanted to die.

But in the warmth of the carriage and with Vi fussing over her, her pains began to ease. She was relaxed now. Before she had been tense with fear and rage. She even managed to doze a little and only wakened fully when the carriage rattled over cobbles near Stratford church.

She straightened up as they turned into Milton Street. Pockets of fog still haunted doorways. It was not quite dark. They passed the lamp-lighter, with his pole over one shoulder.

"Ask the coachman to stop here," she urged Vi. "I don't want Adrian or his mother to see me in this carriage."

Vi wasn't frightened of the Beattys. "Don't be daft. I can easily say it belongs to a friend of mine. You're going to be taken to the door; you ain't fit to walk."

The shop loomed out of the murk and they heard Adrian's voice raised in anger. Kitty's spirits flagged; she had been hoping he wouldn't be home. She could see him now on the doorstep, brandishing his arms, having an angry exchange with someone who towered over him.

Vi said; "Seems to be some sort of a shindy. Your husband's having a row with another man."

Kitty pushed Vi's arm away and let herself out of the carriage. The sight of the stranger had started her heart pounding. He had his back to her—yet there was something about him. Unfamiliar in an ulster and tweed cap—but unmistakable too. She gave a strangled cry. "Harvey—Harvey—oh, Harvey—"

He turned at the sound of her voice. The brim of his hat cast a shadow over his face, but she saw his mouth set in a grim line. She was aware but ignored Adrian's look of cold rage. She flung herself at Harvey and clasped him tightly round the neck, laughing and crying at the same time.

Gently he disentangled her arms. He said nothing. He turned and walked away.

She ran after him. Adrian tried to prevent her, but she pushed him aside. She was aware of Vi following her, calling her name. It was rich entertainment for the lamplighter.

"Harvey, wait." She caught up with him, breathless. "I thought you were in Australia. Why didn't you write—?"

He was caught in the light from a lamp post. There was anguish and pity in his expression, and something else too that made her heart contract. This wasn't how she had imagined their reunion.

"If only you had had more faith in me. If only you had waited."

She was stung by his accusation. "I thought you were dead."

"And wasted no time in finding someone else to fill my place. If only—"

"If—if—" she said bitterly. "If only I'd got your letter in time. If only you'd taken me with you as I begged. If only—" she couldn't keep it up. "Oh dearest, dearest, don't look like that. I love you—I've never loved anyone but you. Tell me you still love me. Put your arms round me—oh, I do need you so—"

Again he gently disengaged her hands. "It's too late, Kitty. This is your home. You have a husband and you are carrying his child. Go back to him, and forget me. It's the only way."

She stood as if frozen in time hearing only one sentence. *You are carrying his child.* Adrian had not wasted time! She wanted to scream out—'Not his, Harvey—but yours—yours,' but though she opened her mouth no sound came, just a groan as pain went over her in a wave of turbulence. She doubled up beneath its onslaught and had a hazy idea that Harvey reached out to her. But it was Vi's arms which grabbed her and Vi's stormy voice was the last sound she heard.

"Leave her be. She don't need you, she's got us. We'll take care of her. Leave her with us. Leave her in peace."

TEN

Kitty's son was born at two minutes past midnight, much to Vi's relief when she heard the news. Kitty herself was past caring. For several hours she had suffered such torment that by the end she was too weak to feel anything but a desire to sleep. When it was all over and Mrs Lacey, a neighbour who 'obliged' on such occasions, had sponged her and helped her into a clean night-gown, Dr Rogers said; "it's a good thing your baby was premature. A full-term infant could have killed you."

The doctor's face was grey with fatigue. He had worked as hard as Kitty during the past three hours. He patted her on the head as if she had been a good girl and needed encouragement.

"A puny infant, but that's to be expected—he'll soon fatten up. He's been through it too, you know, look at his

116

poor little head. But don't worry, that swelling will go down in a few days. It's a caput, caused by pressure where he got jammed. You little things with boys' hips weren't built for babies. Now get all the sleep you can and I'll come in to see you tomorrow."

She did not see Adrian until the following afternoon. She had slept all morning and was now propped up in bed with a plate of gruel. Mrs Lacey left the room as soon as Adrian entered.

Kitty looked up, then down again quickly. Not from shame or remorse though she felt both but because the sight of him came as a shock. She had never seen him looking so ill. His skin was more yellow, his eyes more staring, a vein throbbed in his temple, and he bit nervously on his bottom lip. She marvelled that he was able to control his feelings as well as he did.

He looked down at her broodingly. "So now we have the truth of it. You planned to pass your bastard off as a seven-month premature. I might have swallowed that— but four months! Oh no. So what little ploy are you going to pull out of that scheming little mind now?"

She would have preferred his anger to this clumsy sarcasm. There was no point in trying to answer him. She leant back on her pillow and shut her eyes and she heard him go away. He kept away for another week—so did his mother. Mrs Lacey prepared her meals and attended to her.

One afternoon Kitty had fallen asleep while feeding the baby. She awoke suddenly to find Adrian watching her. Blushing, she brought the sheet up over herself and the sleeping child. Adrian looked tired and he spoke in a weary monotone.

"There is no question of a divorce, I wouldn't give you the satisfaction. But I also know I can't prevent you leaving me to go to your lover—that is if he still wants you."

117

The barb went home. She flinched.

"Does he know about your—your—?" he couldn't bring himself to say the word 'son'.

"He thinks the baby is yours."

It was his turn to flinch and again he left abruptly. He left her alone for three days after that. She took delight in watching her baby thrive. The signs of his difficult birth began to fade, the tiny wrinkles in his neck and wrists to fill out. She looked eagerly for likenesses to Harvey, but there were none. If anything he looked a tiny miniature of her father and this amused and hurt her at the same time. She was so homesick for her family. She wanted Harvey. She tried not to fret. Mrs Lacey had warned her that fretting would dry up her milk.

When Adrian came to see her for the third time he was altogether more composed. He sent Mrs Lacey downstairs to make some tea, then drew up a chair beside her bed. Kitty was wearing a pink knitted bedjacket Maggie had sent. Her hair hung down in two plaits. She had no idea how motherhood had added an extra bloom to her beauty. Adrian eyed her hungrily, thinking she had never looked so desirable. He had to look away, to try to keep cool or he would never have been able to make the speech he had carefully prepared.

"I've been talking things over with my mother. Taking in consideration your youth, and shall we say, a foolish infatuation with a man who took advantage of you—we are prepared to overlook your—um—misfortune. The fault is not all yours. If I had been more understanding, or my mother more charitable, you might have confided in us." (Kitty couldn't believe her ears). "This doesn't mean to say we condone what has happened, but we are prepared to forgive. I want you to understand that I am still willing to give you the security of a home and a position as my wife—but on conditions, of course. You can't expect me to father another man's child. It will either have to go to a home, or alternatively, now that your sister is married, she might have it."

Kitty glared. "*It*, as you keep calling my son, is a human being. Not a parcel to be left in any convenient place. As soon as I'm well enough to travel—as soon as Dr Rogers says I may—I'm taking him back to Falmouth. To his father, and I shall stay with his father whether you divorce me or not. I never thought of you as my husband, anyway. In the eyes of God I am Harvey's wife."

"Don't talk drivel, woman." Adrian got up and began to pace the room. "Supposing your precious Harvey isn't waiting for you in Falmouth. That made you wince, didn't it! Who will keep you then? You'll come running back to me soon enough."

"Never."

"Kitty, listen to me. I haven't been the best of husbands I know. But give our marriage another chance. Once you've got over this feeling for that other fellow—found a home for his child—we can start all over again, have children of our own." He ignored her deliberate shudder. "I was wrong to bring you back to this wretched little shop. We'll move—somewhere out in the country like Woodford or Chingford. A new house with a bath-room and a garden. How would you like that? Kitty, look at me."

She did. "I'd rather go on the streets than ever be your wife again."

He went ashen. "You're going the right way about it," he said. As he got to the door Mrs Lacey came through with the tea. He pushed her to one side. "Out of my way. Damn you, woman!"

Mrs Lacey put her tray on the wash-stand. "Proper gentleman, I don't think. Don't let him upset you, dear. Here, have a nice cup of hot tea, and here's a letter to cheer you up."

It was a note, delivered by hand. Mrs Lacey made a

reliable go-between. She had smuggled out letters to Harvey and to Vi. This was Vi's answer.

"I tried to see you but that old witch, your mother-in-law, wouldn't let me bye. I had flours and a present for the baby, but she wouldn't take them. We want you to no that if things get to much for you, there's always a home for you hear. Come to us for Christmas. There won't be much piece on earth where you are. Send a message by Mrs Lacey. Give the baby a kiss for us.

Much love,
Vi."

Kitty had already sounded Dr Rogers out about going back to Cornwall before Christmas, but he wouldn't hear of it. "Nonsense—madness. A premature infant—this weather—ask me again in the New Year."

However, he thought the idea of spending Christmas with friends in Nelson Street a good one. "At least it will give you a respite," he said, not qualifying his remark, knowing Kitty understood what he meant. He even offered to drive her over. How he got permission from the Beattys he didn't say. Since Mrs Lacey left, Kitty had been under siege. She could not go out as she had no carriage to wheel baby in, and the others came nowhere near her. She would wait until she heard her mother-in-law go into the shop and the street door close on Adrian, then she would go downstairs and collect all she needed for the day. It meant that most of her meals were cold, though she did manage a hot drink at least twice a day. After two weeks of living like this the humble little house in Nelson Street seemed like a sanctuary.

"Pull your chair up to the fire, love," said Ma Watling, taking the baby from Kitty and drooling over him. "Isn't he a darlin' little fella then—ain't he a lamb. Being Christmas Eve Vi will be late tonight. After the Cascade closes she's going down Angel Lane to get the turkey. They sells them off cheap after midnight. 'Ope she brings in something for our supper."

Vi didn't disappoint them. She came home with three smoked haddocks large enough to overlap their plates. Kitty ate hers like one on the verge of starvation.

"Can't beat that place in Angel Lane for 'addicks," said Ma, her mouth full.

Kitty hummed to herself as she helped to prepare the Christmas dinner. She wasn't totally happy but near enough to feel high spirited. It was so wonderful to feel *secure* again. She was still young enough to live only for the moment. Her baby was well, her own health was improving daily, she was among friends—and somewhere in the not too far distant future there was Harvey.

They exchanged presents while they waited for dinner. Hers were modest, purchased for her by Mrs Lacey. A velvet pin-cushion for Ma and a pair of bone-handled hat pins for Vi. In return she received gifts which overwhelmed her. Two hand-stitched flannel night-gowns for the baby from Ma Watling, and from Vi a cashmere shawl as fine as silk. "For Boy's christening," said Vi laconically. For Kitty a plush hat trimmed with a black feather.

"Oh Vi—this must have taken every penny of your wages!"

"Oh, shut up. Go on, let's see you in it."

It was a fetching little headpiece that made Kitty's eyes sparkle with delight when she saw herself in it. Then she removed it with a sigh.

"It's lovely, Vi. But I can't wear it, not just yet."

"Why not, for God's sake?"

"Because it's red, and I'm still in mourning."

"It ain't red. It's plum colour and that's as near as makes no difference to purple which is half-mourning, anyway. It's just an excuse. You don't like it."

"Darling Vi, I do—I do. It's the prettiest hat I've ever had, and you're a dear, kind, generous soul—"

121

"There now, see what you've done, Vi, you've made 'er cry." Ma Watling reached for the whisky bottle. "Come on, girls, stop bickering. Let's 'ave a little bit of Christmas cheer."

By the time dinner was over it was four o'clock. Vi lit the gas and drew the curtains, and they brought their chairs nearer the fire. In a corner Kitty's son slept in the old baby carriage Ma had scoured in readiness. A tiny tuft of reddish hair was all that was visible. Vi cracked nuts with her teeth and passed them round. Ma heated a poker until it was red hot and put it in turn into three glasses of stout. "Come on, love, drink up," she admonished Kitty. "It warms the cockles of yer 'eart, and it's good for nursing mothers, ain't it, Vi?"

"I don't know, I've never nursed one," and Vi laughed so much she choked on a piece of nut.

When the nuts were finished Vi disappeared into the kitchen. When she returned she carried a plate of apples and oranges cut in halves.

"I couldn't manage another thing," said Kitty.

"Come on, it's Christmas. It's only once a year we have a blow-out like this, so make the most of it." Vi took a bite out of her orange and spat the pips into the hearth. "When are you going to give that child a name? You can't go on calling him Boy for ever."

"I want Harvey to choose. After all, he should have a say in the naming of his own son."

"You sure he'll be in Falmouth waiting for you then?"

"Oh yes. He'd have got my letter by now. I wrote as soon as I was well enough, and I explained everything—about why I married Adrian, I mean. I sent the letter to Maggie; she'll know where to find him."

"He hasn't answered?"

"I told him not to. Not to Milton Street, I couldn't be sure I'd get it." Firelight flickered in Kitty's face. She had such a look of beatification that Vi, who had been about to say something else, changed her mind and scowled at Ma instead.

Shortly after Christmas Dr Rogers reluctantly gave his permission for Kitty to travel to Cornwall. He knew that she and the baby were straining the accommodation in Nelson Street and that nothing would induce her to return to the Beattys. Kitty did go to Milton Street, once, on the eve of her journey, to collect some of her things. Adrian waylaid her.

"So you are really leaving?"

She nodded. He looked much thinner. He held out something to her and to her surprise she saw it was a railway ticket.

"Your return fare to Falmouth."

She flushed. "You are so certain I'm coming back then."

"Not certain—just hopeful. Please think over what I've said. If things don't turn out as you hoped, come back again."

"Minus my child, I presume."

"I didn't think you could be so bitter."

"I've had good teachers." She wished she could feel sorry for him, even guilty for making him look so ill, but the only thought uppermost was to get away as quickly as possible. "I realize I must have cost you quite a bit when I had my baby." She wasn't being ironic, she sincerely meant what she said. "I will refund you, every penny." But Adrian misunderstood.

"Was it necessary to twist the knife?" They were the last words he spoke to her. It was only when she was outside again she remembered she had not made any arrangements about having her trunk sent on.

"I'll get Maggie to write," she thought. She was honest enough to realize that most of the dislike she felt for Adrian was born of her own guilt. She still held the ticket in her hand. She didn't want to be beholden to him. She turned to post it through the letter-box, but common-sense prevailed. She hadn't much money left and there'd be expenses on the journey. She pocketed the ticket along with her pride telling herself that one day she would wipe off all her debts to Adrian.

Vi came to see her off. It was an emotional leave-taking.

"You will write—you promise? Ma'll be looking out for every post."

"Of course I'll write, and don't you forget to telegraph Maggie. Let her know what time the train gets to Falmouth."

Vi lifted Boy's veil and kissed the tiny screwed-up face.

"He begins to look more like a little chimp every day! Oh, don't look like that, girl, you know I didn't mean it. He's perfect; of course he's perfect! Well, go on if you're going, I hate bawling in public."

Kitty took a corner seat so that she could wave good-bye, but Vi walked away without once looking back. A whistle blew, the guard waved his flag, steam spurted from the engine's valve, and a plume of smoke lifted to the vaulted roof. The wheels turned—gathered speed—the platform began to slide away. Boy snuffled and squirmed in her arms. A long, tedious journey lay ahead of her, but that mattered little. She was leaving London for ever; she was going home.

Dave was waiting for her at Falmouth station. He welcomed her with the slow shy smile she remembered so well, but in other ways he had changed. He looked older—a man with worries. Boy had lain like a dead weight on her arm for the best part of the journey, and she didn't protest when Dave took him from her. Her feet were numb with cold and her head was throbbing but in the half-light she could see the lights from the harbour and feel the fresh salty wind on her face.

"It's so good to be back," she said.

Dave made no reply. He busied himself buttoning his coat over the baby, then picked up her case in his free hand. As they came away from the shelter of the station he walked in front to take the full force of the wind.

Kitty was bubbling over with unasked questions, but this manner of walking made conversation impossible. She hoped it was only her imagination that made Dave seem uneasy and constrained in his manner.

The first thing she noticed when she walked into Maggie's small living-room was her letter to Harvey, unopened, propped against the clock on the mantelpiece. Her heart gave a leap of fear, then settled into an uneven beat. Her mouth went dry.

Maggie made much of Boy. Kissing him, crowing over him. The cradle their father had made and which had served them in turn as babies was drawn up near the fire. Only when Boy was tucked up and asleep did Maggie give her attention to Kitty. Kitty felt that she too was putting off the inevitable question.

But Kitty was too tired to talk now, too disheartened even. She allowed Maggie to take off her hat and cloak, chafe her frozen hands and feet, then to bring her a bowl of soup.

Kitty looked round. Dave had gone.

"What about you and Dave?"

Maggie brushed Kitty's cloak, folded it neatly. She held out the little plum-coloured hat looking at it with a professional eye. "We've had our supper."

"And Father?"

"He's round at the Travellers' Arms."

Kitty registered shock. Her father in a tavern! Maggie, seeing her expression, tightened her lips.

"Don't worry—he hasn't taken to drink—there's no money for that. It's warm in the Travellers' Arms. They keep a good fire and there's always someone to talk to—about the old days—about sail."

"How is he now? Has he got over Mother's death?"

Maggie shrugged. She's aged too, thought Kitty, like Dave. Everyone suddenly looks older. Adrian—Dave—now Maggie. How much older did she look herself, she wondered. "He'll never get over that, but he's accepted it. He's not so vague about things. He's got a part-time job, and that helps. He repairs sails for Greenacre."

Dan Greenacre had once been apprenticed to Joseph Tredennick. "I didn't know Dan had set up on his own," said Kitty.

"Only in a small way, but he's got something Father always lacked; initiative." There was a defeatist note in Maggie's tone. She didn't voice what Kitty was thinking. That Harvey had been the initiative behind their father, and when he left the business collapsed. Thinking of Harvey brought Kitty's mind back to her letter.

"You didn't send my letter on to Harvey."

Maggie slumped down in the chair opposite. "It came too late. He'd already left Falmouth. I hadn't the heart to tell you."

"But—but I wrote as soon as I could. After the baby was born, I mean."

"You don't understand. He didn't return to Falmouth after going down to London to find you. He didn't attempt to get in touch again."

They pieced their different stories together. Harvey had turned up in Falmouth in early November. He had found out that Maggie was now married and sought her out to ask about Kitty. His sudden appearance had come as a shock because all believed he was in Australia. He had briefly told Maggie his story. His travelling companion John Arrowsmith had died of typhoid on the journey to Durban. There Harvey had left the *Aero* thinking it his duty to return to England and break the news to John's people.

What of his duty to me, thought Kitty rebelliously.

From Liverpool he'd come by coaster to Falmouth. He was still fired with dreams of finding gold in Australia. But now he hoped Kitty would marry him and risk the life of a prospector's wife.

Bitterly Kitty interrupted. "Why did he think it suitable to take me on a six-months' voyage to the other side of the world, but wouldn't even consider taking me to America with him?"

"If both you and Harvey had sailed on the *Eugenie* as you wanted, you'd be dead."

"He wasn't to know that. He wouldn't take me to America because he said the future was too uncertain. What about the future in the Australia out-back! Had he thought of that?"

"Kitty, I can't answer for the workings of Harvey's mind. Perhaps during these last eight months he's come to miss you more than he thought he would. Perhaps he discovered he made a mistake not taking you with him in the first place. It's all in the past now, anyway." Maggie's voice betrayed the fact that she cared little either way. She was too weary.

"So you told him I had married Adrian?"

"What else could I do."

"You didn't tell him about the baby?"

"No. I thought that had to come from you."

"Oh Maggie, if only you had. He wouldn't have walked off that night then without me."

"I don't know, Kitty. I honestly don't know."

"And he didn't come back to Falmouth?"

"Dave made enquiries as soon as we heard from you what had happened. He found out that Harvey had sailed on another Danish ship—again bound for Australia—"

"So he still hasn't given up all dreams of finding gold!" Kitty shivered, partly from cold, partly from the fear that she would never see Harvey again. Boy stirred and began to whimper. Maggie brought him to her and she fed him.

One breast was very painful. Maggie said; "You look ever so tired. Wouldn't you like to go to bed?"

Later Maggie took her upstairs to show her where she was to sleep. "I hope you won't mind sharing a bed with me—like old times. Dave will sleep downstairs—it's only for tonight, anyway." Maggie didn't enlarge on this, and Kitty was barely listening, locked as she was in thoughts of her own. "There's only one other bedroom, very small, where Father sleeps." She left Kitty to settle Boy in the cradle they had carried upstairs and to unpack her few things.

The bedroom was freezing. Boy was warm enough in his cocoon of flannels and shawls, but Kitty's hands grew numb as she began to unpack. Her head ached with a dull persistent pain and though she shivered she felt strangely hot. She supposed she had caught a chill on the journey.

The staircase led straight into the living-room. She felt her way down step by step, making no sound and surprised Maggie at the table, her head buried in her arms sobbing with a kind of wild abandon. Kitty was beside her at once, her arms round her.

Maggie lifted her head and turned away as if ashamed of her tears. "I didn't mean you to see me like this. Suddenly everything got on top of me. Seeing you in that expensive little hat, I thought somehow things had improved for you. I even considered asking whether you could let me have my five pounds back. Then I saw you were still wearing Mother's old skirt, and I saw the cracks in your boots. Oh, Kitty, this has been the worst winter of my life. I sometimes haven't known where our next meal was coming from."

Out it all came—her pent-up misery—the shame and degradation of poverty—the niggling ways to save every penny. Kitty now understood why Dave and her father spent most evenings in the local tavern. There, there was warmth. At home, after tea, Maggie let the fire die down, going to bed early to keep warm. But this was but a small thing. Her greatest anxiety was over Dave's future.

The pilchard industry had been going through a bad time. In times past Dave had got by during such periods by doing odd jobs in different boat-yards. Now there was too much competition for such jobs.

"He's decided to go up north to St. Just's," said Maggie, her voice dulled by despair. "He hopes to find work in the tine mines. He leaves tomorrow morning."

"Oh Maggie, not the mines—not Dave. He's been at sea since he was a boy. Going down a mine will kill him."

Maggie rose. She pushed a piece of loose hair from her eyes. "There's more than one way of dying. I can't watch a strong man sitting here day after day feeling useless because he has nothing to do—*that* would kill him. He's made up his mind, there's nothing I can say. The money is good and he'll be home once a month," she caught her breath. "I shall miss him. He's a good man—a kind husband."

"And now I've landed myself on you—an extra mouth to feed. Oh Maggie, what a mess. I wish I could die."

"You wicked girl to say such a thing, I could shake you. And you with that innocent little love upstairs dependent on you. You're tired—we're both tired, we've talked enough for one night. Off to bed with you. I'll be up as soon as I've made up the couch for Dave."

That night Kitty began to run a fever. In her delirium she called over and over for Harvey. Maggie spent most of the night douching her with cold compresses. In the morning she sent Dave, before he caught his train, for the doctor.

Mastitis was the diagnosis. "You'd know it better as milk fever," said the doctor. Maggie was told that the baby would have to be weaned immediately and the patient treated with magnesium sulphate compresses and hot fomentations. For three days Kitty was very ill and

Maggie hardly stirred from her bedside. Kind neighbours took it in turn to relieve her. One, a young married woman with a three-week old baby, took Boy off her hands completely. "I've got more than enough milk for two. There, there, me poor handsome," she dropped a kiss on the top of Boy's head. "You come along o' me."

At the end of the week the doctor declared Kitty out of danger. "In spite of what she's been through, she's a healthy girl. She's got a strong constitution and she's got youth on her side. But she'll need careful nursing for a week or two yet."

When the doctor had gone Maggie broke down and wept from relief and exhaustion. Kitty's illness had taken its toll of her too. Then she went upstairs to see if Kitty was awake.

She was hardly recognizable from the girl who had arrived just a week ago. Maggie, from the best of intentions, had cropped her hair close to her head. It had been impossible to brush it when Kitty was at the height of her fever. Her face looked so small without the thick braids and her eyes enormous, like those in the face of a child dying of malnutrition. She was too weak to talk. She put out her hand and Maggie grasped it. She had never loved her younger sister more than at that moment.

Kitty made a slow recovery, but illness had changed her. As her mother would have said; 'One does not ride through the valley of the shadow of death without paying something towards the fare.' Once assured that her baby was thriving in the care of his foster mother, she did not ask for him again, and never mentioned Harvey. The question of the baby's baptism arose and Kitty said she would name him after her father and Dave. Her first outing after her illness was to the little chapel on the hill where Joseph David was named at the font and Maggie, Dave and their father were godparents. It was soon after this that Kitty talked about returning to Adrian.

"I think things will be different between us in future, at least I hope so. I'll have to leave little Joe with you, Maggie, but I'm sure I can get round Adrian to make me an allowance and I'll send you every penny I can spare."

"What makes you think Adrian will change?"

"He was—even before I left. I think in his odd fashion he loves me. If I can be a proper wife to him, give him the children he wants—"

"But I thought you said there was something the matter with him. Some hereditary trait—"

Kitty smiled a bitter little smile. "That is what Dr Rogers said. He could be mistaken; that's a risk I should have to take. That's something Adrian and I will have to decide between ourselves." Her new-found maturity went at odds with her waif-like appearance. Maggie ducked her head against the sleeping baby she was nursing.

"I wish you could stay here."

"No more than I do, but how can I? Where is the room? Where is the money to keep me and little Joe? Could I find work? Not here—I'd be better off at home," and as she said the word 'home' a vision of the Milton Street shop came to her and she felt sick with an awful disquiet.

Later on she said; "If Harvey should ever return to Falmouth I don't want him to know that Joe is his son. Pretend I had to leave him behind for health reasons; anything you like—but never let him know the truth."

"But Kitty—"

Kitty's eyes glinted coldly. "I couldn't keep his trust. I don't want his pity. Spare me that, Maggie."

Kitty left for London on a February morning that held a promise of spring. Snowdrops were out in many gardens, and early primroses were in bud under the hedges. Kitty turned for a last look at the restless sea. The kittiwakes glided on air currents, noisy, squabbling beautiful birds. The noise they made sounded like a

131

lament. They're keening for me, thought Kitty despairingly.

She was dry-eyed when she kissed little Joe good-bye. She shook hands with her father who insisted on carrying her case to the station. He seemed unaware of the emotional maelstrom sucking Kitty away to London. He didn't approve of her leaving her baby behind but he didn't question why.

Maggie hugged her. Kitty's face was impassive, but her own streamed with tears. "It isn't right you going off like this. We could've managed somehow."

"Please Maggie, don't make it any harder for me." She did not stand and wave as the train steamed out of the station this time. She sat down and stared stonily into the middle distance. The bread and cheese Maggie had packed for her remained untouched the entire journey. When she got to Paddington she threw it to the pigeons.

There were no lights visible in the shop in Milton Street. She rang twice before she heard the lagging footsteps of her mother-in-law coming to the door, then bolts being drawn. When the door opened Mrs Beatty peered at her without surprise.

"So you came back. I suppose you'd better come in." She led the way back to the parlour. The frowsty air hit Kitty afresh. The room was in a state of disorder; it looked as if it hadn't been cleaned for days. She loosened her cloak and sat down. Mrs Beatty looked at her cropped hair without a change of expression.

"Is Adrian out?"

Her mother-in-law looked at her in a stupefied manner. "I buried him last Tuesday."

Shock waves went through Kitty. She started up, then sank back again, her legs weak. "For goodness sake, why didn't you let me know? When was he taken ill?"

"He had one of his bad turns again just after you left. He went down to Hastings thinking the sea air might help. He died very sudden. They didn't even have time to send for me."

Kitty sat bemused, now knowing how best to show her sympathy. Her mother-in-law's voice was like a dirge.

"I should have let you know. The people at the hotel said he asked for you at the end. But there were other things on my mind. I thought she would come to the funeral. I went to see her but the house was all shuttered up. Then I remembered—she always went to the South of France for the winter."

"She?"

"Her ladyship—his grandmother. I always thought—I always hoped she would acknowledge him one day. He was her only grandchild. Mind you, she always took an interest in him. She liked him to go and see her every Tuesday, but lately, he told me, she was getting confused, didn't always know him. Well, she was nearly ninety. I wrote to her, but she didn't answer. I didn't expect her to, really. I was nothing to her, just a kitchen-maid once." Her pale protruding eyes stared at Kitty, expressionlessly. "I had such hopes—such dreams—you do hear of it, don't you? She could have made him her heir. I lived for that."

It's incredible, thought Kitty—right up to the last! The toneless voice droned on;

"We didn't treat you right when you first came, Kitty." (It was the first time she had used her name). "I resented you. I thought you were spoiling Adrian's chances of marrying someone better. He did love you, you know. He cried the night you left."

Kitty felt a scream rising up in her throat. "Please, Mrs Beatty, don't say any more. You're only hurting yourself—"

"I was thinking. I suppose you wouldn't come back and live here with me. Bring the baby?"

The old revulsion came back in force. "I couldn't do

133

that."

"No. I didn't really expect you would."

"Will you stay on here alone?"

"Without Adrian's money I can't keep the shop going, and now that he's gone—" the tired voice cracked, struggled for composure. "There won't be any income coming in. I could go and live with my sister in Plaistowe. She's a widow and she never had any family. You will go and see Adrian's grave, won't you? It's a private one. I'm going to have a stone—black marble. He would have liked that."

Even now this obsession with grandeur. It had eaten away her life, emptying it of every thought but the one of Adrian's high-born connections. Empty dreams of what might have been, and now an empty future. Kitty wished she had the moral courage to put her arms round the older woman and comfort her. She got to her feet and put on her cloak.

"Where will you go? Back to Cornwall?"

"I don't think so. I'll go and see my friends in Nelson Street first."

Mrs Beatty nodded. "Friends, yes—that's nice. I never had time for friends myself. Adrian was enough for me." Her pale eyes wandered to Kitty's face. This time they registered. "You've been ill, haven't you? You look very tired. Stay here just tonight. Let me make you a cup of tea."

Kitty felt that if she did not get away she would be caught in a mesh of inertia. She saw in this thin, half-demented woman the outcome of years of frustrated longing. It was too near the bone. It had a parallel in her own obsessive longing for Harvey. She made her excuses, promised to come agaon, and thankfully closed the door behind her.

She stood under a lamp-post looking at her wedding ring, then she slipped it off and put it in her pocket. It signified nothing now. She felt no grief for Adrian, just a sadness for a wasted life. She was Kitty Tredennick again. Nobody ever again would call her Mrs Beatty. And neither would she any longer think of herself as Harvey's natural wife. She was alone except for her son. She would live for him now. She would work—she would save money. One day she would have him back to live with her.

Vi would help. Bruno Chalk had already shown an interest. Forget the Silver Cascade. It was the Golden Cascade and the golden sovereigns that rattled in the till—that was her aim now. She adjusted her cloak against the cold night air and turned in the direction of Nelson Street.

ELEVEN

One September afternoon Kitty sat before her dressing-table in the apartment she shared with Vi on the top floor of the Golden Cascade. The word 'apartment' was really too grand to apply to the large room with a smaller one leading from it, but at least it afforded a privacy much envied by the other resident girls who slept in dormitory-type bedrooms.

The smaller of the two rooms was only adequate to hold the double bed and seven-foot wardrobe, so they kept the dressing-table in the other room which Vi insisted on calling the 'boodwaw'. When Kitty had joined the staff of the Golden Cascade nearly two years pre-viously it had been possible for her to look out of the window of the big room on to the shingled roof of an eighteenth-century coffee-house, but progress in the name of development had demolished the coffee-house along with its neighbours, and now a towering hotel not only obscured her view of Green Park but blocked out the afternoon sun. There were compensations, however. They overlooked one of the bedrooms, and many a human comedy (and sometimes tragedy) had she and Vi witnessed. But at present Kitty was in no mood to feel interest not even when a chambermaid entered the bedroom and began to make it ready for a new occupant.

Vi, coming in in her usual ebullient fashion, broke in on Kitty's thoughts. Two years at the Golden Cascade had had a taming effect on her. She wore more muted colours and no longer hennaed her hair—that had been one of Bruno's stiuplations. Kitty often wished, especially when her head ached, as now, that Vi could also moderate her voice. It was one of the drawbacks which kept her in the bar on the ground floor instead of with Kitty in the gaming-rooms above. But Vi was well content. She had got what she banted—a niche in the West End, and though she knew she was only tolerated because of Kitty, it didn't worry her.

She flung her hat on the sofa and sat down to unbutton her boots.

"You should just see the crowds in Oxford Street—God knows where they all come from. I got a nice piece of green shot-silk in Shepherd's Market. I thought I'd ask Ma Watling to make it up for me, she don't charge as much as they do round here. What about coming over to Stratford with me one day next week?"

"I'll see." Kitty's total lack of interest brought Vi's head up with a jerk. She frowned. Now what was the matter?

The last three years had left their mark on Kitty, had hollowed out her cheeks and left a bruised look to her eyes. Vi knew the reason for it well enough, and when she saw a letter from Maggie crumpled on the dressing-table pin-tray her spirits plummeted. There would be weeping in the small hours tonight, and in spite of a certain impatience her heart ached for this unhappy girl still fretting for her baby.

"What news from Maggie?" she asked with a pretence at indifference which Kitty could see through well enough.

"Nothing but good news—very good news." Why then the brittle edge to Kitty's voice? "As you know Dave is back on the pilchard boats again, and they've had a very good season. They are even thinking of moving—to a new estate. Seven-and-six a week rent, if you please. They couldn't have afforded that a year ago—"

"Why not? Goodness knows you make a generous enough allowance."

Kitty ignored that. Vi's frequent references to the voluntary gratuities Kitty made to her different relatives was a bone of contention between them. "Actually the main reason for the move is that they want somewhere bigger. Maggie is at last expecting. She writes here she hopes for a little girl—*a sister for Joe*!"

So that was the crux of the matter. A sister for Joe, thought Vi savagely—why couldn't Kitty's own sister had used more tact? Didn't she guess at the tug-of-war going on inside her all the time!

Vi recalled with disquiet Kitty's last homecoming from Falmouth six months previously. She had returned from her Easter holiday in a mood that peaked between passion and silence, snapping at anyone who questioned her. Finally she broke down in an anguish bordering on hysteria.

"Little Joe *screamed* at me," she said sobbing, in Vi's arms. "When I tried to cuddle him he arched his back and screamed at me. He calls Maggie mummy. I'm a stranger to him."

Vi had comforted her, rocking her as if she were but a

child too. "It's your money what's keeping him, pet. One day he'll know and be grateful. Think of that."

"I don't want his gratitude, I want his love. Oh Vi, I just want to hear him call me 'mummy', that's all."

Now out of the side of her eye Vi watched in a state of suspense the slight figure of Kitty as she drooped on her stool, turning her hair-brush over and over in her hands. She still wore her hair short and it suited her though it gave her a *gamine* look which contrasted oddly with the stylish gowns she almost always wore.

Vi probed carefully. "Why not ask Bruno if your sister could bring Joe up to London for a spell? We could put them up here and it would be a treat for Maggie. You say she's never seen London—"

Kitty dropped the brush and spun round, glaring; "Bring them here! To this den of vice. You must be mad."

Colour rushed into Vi's cheeks. Her hands began to shake and she clasped them together, not wanting to lose her temper. She controlled her voice with difficulty. "Den of vice—what the hell are you talking about—?"

"You know well enough. The Silver Cascade was tawdry and vulgar in its way, but at least if offered clean family entertainment. But here—you know what goes on here. You're not blind to the little rooms, discreetly hidden away where a gentleman may wine and dine any lady of his choice. You know very well that this place is nothing but an upper-class whore-house—"

Vi's patience snapped. She got to her feet, her eyes blazing, and grabbed Kitty by her shoulders. "You little fool, you don't know what you're talking about. I wish I could shake some sense into you for once. What goes on here is harmless enough—nobody's forced to do anything they don't wanter. You should 'ave seen where I was born. Little brats hardly out of the cradle thieving and scavenging, otherwise they would 'ave starved to death.

Prostitutes of thirteen and fourteen—the younger the better because there was a good market for virgins. That's what I call vice—social vice—and I do know what that means. The only thing really wrong with this place is the gaming-room where you queen it, my love—an' that's only 'cos it's outside the law. One of these days the law will catch up with Bruno Chalk and we'll all be for it then, but until that day comes stop talking about vice in that sanctimonious way 'cos you make me sick!''

Vi stamped out of the room, slamming the door behind her, and Kitty sat on immobile, alarmed at the storm of feeling she had unleased in her friend. She picked up Maggie's letter, tried to straighten it out, got it back into its envelope and put it away in the top drawer of the dressing-table. Of course Vi was right. She fetched a deep sigh. Vi—Maggie—they were always on the side of commonsense; only she blundered on, a victim of her own emotions.

She played with the idea that now Dave was in a better position and not relying on her allowance, she could leave the Golden Cascade. But where would she go? What was she trained for? And Bruno—she owed him a certain loyalty.

After a year behind the bar at the Silver Cascade he had groomed her for Mayfair. She had been taught how to handle a train; how to walk up and down stairs; how to enter and alight from a carriage. He had paid for elocution lessons so that no trace of a Cornish accent remained and above all he had taught her about fashion. In the gaming-rooms she had been trained by the best croupiers and had acquired a self-confidence that enabled her to mix easily with the sophisticated patrons. And yet—oh, that 'yet'—she would gladly exchange all this to be Harvey's 'kitten' once again. Last thing at night she thought of him. Every morning she awakened with the image of his face before her.

She heard a soft rap on the door. Bruno never came in without first knocking; it was one of his little courtesies. He came up behind her and spoke to her reflection.

"Idling on a fine afternoon like this? Come along, put on your wraps. I have something to show you."

She never questioned—always obeyed him. Outside, his carriage was waiting. He handed her in, took his seat beside her, solicitously tucked the lap-robe about her. They bowled along Piccadilly, into Regent Street, across Oxford Circus. London had the tired look of late summer. Already the plane trees were shedding their leaves and dust lay thick like a grey shroud. The sun, slanting on soot-blackened façades, pin-pointed the grim of centuries. Kitty wondered if that was why most people wore such dark clothes.

She herself was dressed in navy foulard and a close-fitting hat swathed in pink tulle. She knew it was becoming, had been aware of Bruno's appraisal. He paid for all her clothes. It was part of the job—he said.

The carriage turned into a square and stopped, the coachman obviously having had instructions. There were few bystanders. It was too late for afternoon callers, too early for evening jaunts. Pigeons strutted amidst horses' droppings, pecking at bits of straw. Kitty saw that one of the houses had an empty, shuttered look and a board advertised its lease for sale. It looked familiar and she suddenly remembered.

"Good Heavens—this is the house my husband showed me. Where he was born—"

"Yes. I saw the announcements of the owner's death and remembered what you had told me about her. Some quirk of fancy made me want to see your husband's birthplace. Quite impressive."

"As far as garrets go!"

He ignored that. "Would you like me to purchase the lease, for you, I mean?"

"If that's a joke, I'm not amused."

"Come, my dear, why should I be joking? How would you like to be mistress of such a fine property? Doesn't the irony appeal to you?"

There was a gleam in his eye she didn't trust. Was she being over-sensitive or had he stressed the word 'mistress'? As to the irony in the situation, it was to him it appealed, not to herself. She still flinched from anything that reminded her of Adrian.

"I'd prefer a cottage in Falmouth," she said truthfully.

He laughed. "You never disappoint me—always the unexpected retort. Don't dismiss my proposition too quickly. I'm serious."

But was he? He was a man of unpredictable moods, and this was not the first time he had made such suggestions to her. She was aware that the staff at the Golden Cascade already looked upon her as his mistress, and there was conjecture among some of the guests. It had hurt at first, but she had soon grown another skin. One couldn't live and work at the Cascade without doing so.

She sometimes looked back with nostalgia at her apprenticeship at the Silver Cascade. She had had a lively boisterous time there working at the bar with Vi; and a comfortable retreat in Nelson Street. She had gone through devastating bouts of depression in the early days mourning for Joe, but Ma and Vi had learnt how to cope and soon jollied her out of her suffering. Now, nearly three years afterwards, outwardly she had everything. Beautiful clothes, all the trappings of a life of comfort. But there was still something missing—it was peace of mind.

It was time to change when they returned to the Golden Cascade. Dusk was filling the streets and the lamps on the carriages made her think of eyes forever searching after lost ways. She liked London best by lamp-light. Its many scars were invisible then; the gas jets gave it a softer, cleaner look.

Vi was already in the bar, giving her orders, chivvying the messenger-boys. She caught Kitty's eye and grinned, giving her the thumb's-up sign. The storm was over.

Mrs Mudie, one of the dressers, helped Kitty out of her foulard and put out the gown she was to wear that evening. She then went off to run Kitty's bath. The light was on in the hotel bedroom and Kitty noticed the bed had been turned down. She had had her bath and was sitting in her dressing-gown buffing her nails when Bruno knocked again.

"Sitting in the dusk? Here, let me light the gas."

"No—I like it as it is. There's enough light from the street."

"Have you been crying, my dear?"

"No!"

"Ah, that was just a little too quick. A pity, I want you to look your best tonight. We are being patronized by royalty—"

"Not the—"

He chuckled. "Oh no, just a very minor German prince, but the first time royalty has ever visited the Golden Cascade so we must make the most of it. Which gown are you wearing?"

"My grey taffeta—the one patterned with parma violets."

"Very nice. Very suitable for a church sociable. But I think something more adventurous for tonight. Your green velvet?"

"Why not the red? Then I could be called the scarlet woman with some truth!"

This time her retort did not amuse him. "Sarcasm does not become you. Now please hurry."

"I must ring for Mrs Mudie—"

"I will hook you up."

When she came out of the bedroom she saw that he had

lit the small gilt lamps on the dressing-table. It stood out, brightly illuminated, just by the window, leaving the rest of the room in shadow. As he was hooking the back of her gown his fingers against her bare flesh trembled slightly. On her account? Cynically she dismissed such an idea. The thought of royalty more than likely.

She looked at her reflection critically. "I don't like this gown—it is too low."

"I have something to rectify that. Sit down again, my dear." She watched as he drew a leather case from his pocket. He opened it and she saw the sparkle of jewels. She gasped as he lifted to her view a necklace of flawless emeralds.

"For me! They must be worth a fortune."

"They are, and that is why you must return them to me at the end of the evening. They are only on loan—bait for His Highness of course—" She saw the gleam of his teeth and knew he was grinning. He gave her neck a gentle push and she inclined her head so that he could do up the clasp. The stones felt cold against her flesh and she shivered. "A perfect neck for such baubles," he whispered, and his lips moved slowly over her neck to the hollow in her collarbone before she pulled away sharply. His behaviour brought back memories she wanted to forget. Even the smell of his bay rum and aroma of cigars, reminded her forcibly of Adrian.

"So sorry, my dear," he said blandly. "I didn't know you were ticklish."

But she didn't hear. Her attention had been caught by movements in the room opposite. A chambermaid was placing a brass can of hot water on the wash-stand and immediately behind her stood a man. He came to the window looking out. It was too dark to see his features, the light was behind him; but something in the set of his head, the breadth of his shoulders, caused her to stiffen. She must have made some sort of noise for Bruno said;

"What is it, Kitty? What made you gasp?"

She shivered. "I felt cold. I expect it's a draught from the window. Would you draw the curtains, please?"

TWELVE

Kitty let herself into the casino before the first of the evening guests arrived. This was the hour which she liked best, when all was quiet, the lights low; then the gaming-rooms held a certain attraction for her. The thick carpets, the plush hangings, the gilt and crystal chandeliers, the polished wood—all enhanced the muted excitement engendered by the power of money. Money to be won—money to be lost—money to be staked. Here she had witnessed hearts broken, liaisons started, heirlooms lost, fortunes found. When the guests arrived, all would be a kaleidoscope of colour—of rich silks and furs and jewels. But for this one moment she had it all to herself. She laid her hand on one of the blackjack tables. She had started here as a croupier before being promoted to the title of hostess.

Hostess was an ambiguous word—a word Bruno had brought over from America. Some of the male patrons took it for something quite different, but a quiet word from Bruno soon disillusioned them. It was an enviable rôle. They were provided with beautiful clothes; they were obliged to behave impeccably, at least during working hours. Bruno was not interested in how they behaved in their own time as long as they did not discredit the Golden Cascade.

Kitty had earned the title of Lady Luck, for luck always attended the man who could persuade her to escort him. For a time Kitty got some satisfaction from this strange power—she had no idea she possessed—until one day, one of the head croupiers, or *Chef de Table* as Bruno preferred them to be called, enlightened her. It was possible to rig the roulette wheel, and at a nod from Bruno, they sometimes did. Kitty realized then that Bruno always picked her partners—someone he wanted to oblige? Or from whom he wanted a future favour? Her self-esteem took a knock to the benefit of her cynicism.

Vi came through the folding doors which led to the main staircase. "I just had to come up to see if you're all right." Her eyebrows shot up at the sight of the emeralds. She went to say something, but seeing Kitty's expression thought better of it. "What's happened?"

"I believe I've seen Harvey."

"You're imagining things, girl. You couldn't 'ave—-he's in Australia."

"Someone just like him came into the hotel bedroom. It was Harvey, I know it was—and he looked straight at me."

Vi came nearer to give her a closer look. "Here, you'd better pull yourself together before the gamers come." She always called them gamers—never clients or patrons or guests. "Come down to the bar and 'ave a tot. You've got time."

147

Kitty made an impatient gesture—that was Vi's panacea for everything. Heartache—heartburn—chills—nerves—fright—the overall magic cure. Then Kitty softened—there was real concern in Vi's voice.

"It *was* Harvey, you know. And he must have seen Bruno kissing my neck—"

"Oh my God, you do choose your moments, don't you? But do you care? Do you really care?"

"You know I do, Vi. I don't want him to think I—that Bruno—Well, anyway I bet you he comes here tonight. I bet you anything you like."

"Look dearie, just remember one thing—you don't belong to nobody. Nobody don't own you—you can do what you like. I've admired you so these past few years, you've been such a little fighter. Don't go all soft now just because that man's come back—or you think he's come back. I'd better go. They're beginning to come in."

She gave Kitty a hasty kiss, touched the emeralds and deliberately winked and left with a loud crash of the door. Kitty winced. Her head throbbed more than ever.

The croupiers were arriving in twos and threes. The other hostesses moved around, touching the feathers or flowers in their hair, bunching a bustle that may have got flattened. They smiled in turn at Kitty giving covert glances at her emeralds. She fancied they whispered about her behind their fans.

Bruno arrived, gliding in that fussy way of his to her side. He scrutinized her keenly. "You're looking rather flushed. Perhaps too much rouge?"

"You know I never wear rouge."

He smiled dismissively, already his thoughts running ahead to the evening before them. He began to fidget among the tables, removed a hair from one of the croupiers shoulders, picked up a fallen leaf from a flower arrangement. His actions tore at Kitty's nerves and she wished he would just stand still and relax.

With the first arrivals his mood changed. He was brisk, attentive, the perfect host. An hour passed, then another. Kitty sensed Bruno's growing apprehension and wondered why he attached so much importance to this minor foreign prince. A sudden commotion at the entrance told her when the moment had come. She saw a tall man with waxed moustaches in a white uniform glittering with gold braid and prepared to make her curtsey, but he was only the equerry. The prince was a shrunken little man with white hair, in a well-worn tail coat.

Bruno bowed, at his most unctuous. "Your Royal Highness, may I present my ward, Miss Kitty Tredennick?" Faded eyes in a network of wrinkles twinkled at her and her nervousness waned. She was prepared to like this timid-looking little man, until as she walked away with him, she felt his hand caressing her thigh, and realized then she had been encumbered with what Vi would have called 'a randy old goat'. But this was one of the disadvantages of an extremely well-paid job.

"You choose, my pretty," he answered when she asked whether he wanted to play roulette or blackjack. His hand fumbled for her buttock but was thwarted by her bustle. She swayed away from him, leading the way to Table Four.

Room was made for them, then the circle of spectators closed round them again. Under the table the prince stroked Kitty's knee. She hoped that in the excitement of winning his interest in her would lessen.

The *chef de table* had had his instructions. The chips in front of the prince began to mount and the murmurs of the onlookers increased. Kitty was free to look around her, to watch the door. All evening she had been waiting for an entrance too.

It was nearly midnight; she was beginning to wonder if she had mistaken the figure in the bedroom, when in he came, pausing on the threshold looking about him with a detached, somewhat superior manner—her Harvey. Taller than she remembered him, carrying more weight, his hair bleached to the colour of pale gold and his skin many shades darker. Her heart swelled with longing and loving, and another sensation that wasn't altogether pleasant.

She knew he was seeking her out. The grey eyes swept every table in turn—inexorably they found her, then deliberately focused on the emeralds. There was a perceptible quizzical lifting of his brows.

Kitty raised her chin, forcing herself to meet the overt insinuation with defiance when all the time her heart told her to run to him and clasp him in her arms. A rowdy party, being discreetly escorted to the exit, obscured her vision. Mentally she brushed them impatiently aside. When next she saw the blond head rising above its neighbours, it was making for the next table.

For the next half an hour she watched him losing money in a reckless manner. Either he had so much it didn't matter—or he didn't care either way whether he lost or won. But she did. It was for money, or lack of it, that he had left her in the first place.

The prince was now so engrossed in winning that he merely nodded when Kitty made her excuses, not taking his eyes from the table. Kitty made her way with difficulty through the press of bystanders; it was just as difficult to make a passage through to Harvey's table. She stood just behind him, and in a moment or two caught the eye of the head croupier and nodded to him. He stared back, puzzled, then looked about him for confirmation from Bruno; but Bruno was already commiserating with the prince whose winning streak had suddenly ended.

Again Kitty caught the eye of the croupier and made her meaning very clear. He shrugged; shortly afterwards Harvey began to win back all that he had lost. The spectators drifted from the next table to watch—

150

excitement grew tense; everybody loves a winner, thought Kitty angrily.

She was so close to Harvey she could have touched his hair. It gleamed silkily in the light from the chandelier. Surely he must hear her heart beating? But he played on—no longer reckless but with a grim determination to recoup every penny, not realizing that another nod from her and he would lose it all again.

Bruno came hurrying up, suave on the surface but as Kitty was well aware, raging inwardly. He had a word with the *chef de table*, they both looked at Kitty. The roulette-wheel whirled to a stop.

"No more bets on this table. Will all players please go to Table Three" said the croupier. The players drifted away. Harvey stood up and pocketed his winnings. Only then was he aware of Kitty. He bowed.

"That is a fine necklace you are wearing, Madam," he said gracelessly. "I wonder how many poor devils lost their fortunes to pay for it."

The blood drained from Kitty's face. Harvey's face became a blur as stinging tears filled her eyes. She would not give him the satisfaction of seeing her break down. She turned with a swish of skirts and swept out of the room.

She kept her dignity intact for the length of the corridor, then she gave in and began to cry as she groped for the door to her room. To see Harvey again, to hear his voice—once she would have gone down on her knees thanking God for such a chance—now she wished to Heaven he had not come back. At least, not that well-dressed stranger with the accusing eyes.

She paced to an fro wringing her hands. Wishing one moment she had stayed to fling Harvey's imputation back in his teeth; glad the next to be alone to give vent to her feelings. When the knock came on the door she shouted 'Go away', thinking it was a messenger from Bruno

151

summoning her back to the gaming-rooms.

But it was Harvey who entered. She quickly wiped her eyes with the back of her hand. "How—how did you know this was my room?"

"I worked it out from my vantage point opposite. It wasn't difficult." He was smiling, but it was an affected smile. His voice was expressionless. She suspected that his feelings were as raw as hers but that he had his in better control.

"Nice little nook you've got here. A great improvement on your last one, if you don't mind me saying so."

"How did you find me?"

"Through Maggie, of course."

"So you've been back to Falmouth."

"Yes." He snapped the word at her, showing a crack in his defences.

"I had a letter from Maggie today. She didn't mention you."

"I asked her not to."

So—there was nothing she could say to that. Maggie seemed to be a repository for all secrets. It is ridiculous, thought Kitty, standing here engaging in small talk. This is my lover, the father of my son. Why can't I talk to him naturally? She groped backwards until she came to a chair and sat down, not sure that her legs would support her much longer. Harvey took a chair opposite, crossed his legs and folded his arms, his eyes intent on hers.

"I gather by your appearance that you found gold prospecting successful?"

"You could say that."

"So you are now a rich man?"

"Some might think so."

Oh God, this was awful—he was mocking her. Nervously she put her hand to her throat, and the emeralds, forgotten for the moment, jangled at her touch, and Harvey made a gesture at them; "And you too have made a fortune."

"I've made no fortune—I'm just a working girl," she said crisply.

He startled her the way he bounded out of his chair and came across to her, grasping her by her wrists. "Working girl! Working as what—Chalk's mistress!"

"How dare you. He's my employer—"

"Employer," he mimicked. "Employer. Don't lie to me—"

"I'm not lying. Ask Vi—ask my friend. She's downstairs in the bar—she shares these rooms with me."

His grip was hurting. She struggled to break free but he held her like a vice. All pretence at indifference had gone. There was a savage look on his face, and a vein throbbed in his forehead. "What made you come to a place like this? Why didn't you return to Falmouth when your husband died?"

She was too stunned to answer. The last three years rolled away and she was back in Falmouth, hungry and cold, Maggie crying, her father a broken man, Dave going off to work in the tin mines. All that she had wiped away like wiping a slate clean. By working, saving every penny, sending what she could spare to Maggie, she had helped to raise them out of their poverty, had tided them over until better times. She alone had done that, and done it honestly. And now to hear the accusation in Harvey's voice, to see worse than accusation in his eyes. Something snapped inside her and she wrenched one hand free and with it hit him as hard as she could in the mouth.

He recoiled, taken aback, and she leapt up putting the width of the room between them.

"You sanctimonious hypocrite," she shrieked. "If you only knew what you were saying."

She had left an angry red mark across his mouth. He touched it gingerly. "You don't know your own strength," he laughed, then gave a contemptuous shrug.

"You bought those baubles out of your wages, I presume." He gave another unpleasant laugh. "What is it they say—'the price of a virtuous woman is far above rubies'. Does that also apply to emeralds?"

Neither of them had heard Bruno's knock nor seen him enter. Now he coughed, and they both looked round, startled—almost guiltily. "Guests are not allowed in private apartments," he said in a calculated civil manner. "Would you be good enough to return to the gaming-room?"

"I understood any of the rooms here could be had at a price."

"Not this one."

"What about one of the others then? I would pay handsomely for the company of this young lady."

Kitty drew in her breath. She couldn't bring herself to look any longer at the ugly expression on Harvey's face. She knew he was deliberately goading Bruno, but under-lying it was his contempt for her. Bruno responded with one of his bleak smiles, seeing through Harvey's pretence. "I think your presence here is offensive to Miss Tredennick and I would be obliged if you'd leave," he said quietly.

Harvey looked round at Kitty. Their eyes met for a moment, and she saw that he was deeply hurt. Even then she would have gone to him if he had made the least indication, but he lifted his head with some of his old arrogance and strode swiftly out of the room.

"He's gone. It's all right now," said Bruno when she had stood unmoving for some little while. She sank wearily on to the sofa. "Go and bathe your face and take a stiff brandy. The prince is asking for you."

Kitty stared up at him. The prince—what prince? then she remembered. "Then he can ask till he's blue in the face," she screamed. "Here—when you go, take these with you. They're the cause of all the trouble," and she

154

tugged at the emeralds until they gave way, and flung them across the room.

She didn't see Bruno scuttle after them. She fled into the bedroom and slammed the door after her. Bruno picked up the emeralds and let himself out of the apartment, carefully closing the door behind him. Once in the hallway he took out a handkerchief and mopped hos brow. The girl was mad—she must be mad. Those precious emeralds—and she had *thrown* them at him.

In the early hours of the morning when Vi came to bed she found Kitty asleep but still fully clothed. Gently she eased her out of her gown and between the sheets. She could see she had cried herself to sleep. Poor kid, she thought, and sighed. She hadn't had a very good night herself and her head was aching badly. She went back to the larger room and rested her forehead against the glass of the window, lost for some time in troubled thoughts.

As she straightened up she saw a figure of a man in the hotel room opposite. He was standing at his window looking straight across at her. There was something about his attitude that sent a chill through her. His utter stillness unnerved her. Quickly she drew the curtains together again, turned off the gas, and undressed in the dark.

THIRTEEN

Early the next morning Kitty was summoned to Bruno's office. When the page-boy who brought the message had gone, Kitty glanced uneasily at Vi. Vi, sitting on the sofa darning a stocking, pulled a face. It was no light matter to be summoned to the office. It had happened to Vi, only once, during her early days at the Golden Cascade because she had been acting too freely with one of the waiters.

Kitty found Bruno sitting at his desk chewing on an unlit cigar. He looked tired—preoccupied—but he greeted her quite affably. He motioned her to sit down, and sat watching her, rolling his cigar between his fingers. If his intention was to unnerve her, he was succeeding.

Then he surprised her by asking her if she would like a

holiday. "A long holiday. A month, say, with your sister. You look as if you need it."

She didn't know what to answer. She had expected a reprimand, abuse even—certainly not solicitude. She began to stammer her thanks, but Bruno cut her short.

"I'm doing it for the sake of business, my dear. It wouldn't do the image of the casino much good to have its girls giving the nod for the benefit of ex-lovers. Oh yes, my dear, there's no need to glare at me like that. Most of the staff here have already guessed at the identity of the fortunate young man of last night's little escapade. I'd soon be bankrupt if others took it into their heads to follow your example."

"He only won back his own money."

"Once he lost it, it was no longer his. We are not a charitable institution, my dear." When he said 'my dear' in that tone of voice it became a term of abuse, not affection. Kitty realized she had made a mistake in answering him back and sat in silence awaiting her dismissal. He lit his cigar, inhaled deeply, and leaning back in his chair exhaled at leisure. He squinted at her through the smoke. "I won't say any more about the emeralds. The clasp will have to be mended, of course, but I'll overlook that considering how distraught you were. Well, Kitty," his tone changed. "Away with you, and have a good holiday. Come back with some of your old sparkle. I don't like to see you drooping."

At the door she paused. "You did say a whole month?"

"Longer if need be. I want you back here glowing. The busy season will soon be upon us."

She couldn't believe her good fortune. Her first impulse was to run and tell Vi, but instead she went down to the foyer. It reeked of smoke and stale spirits, odours left over from the previous evening. Cleaning women were polishing the floor and wiping down the plate-glass doors. Kitty passed through the foyer into the theatre. It was small, only about half the size of the one at Stratford and not nearly so elaborate, as if it were but an unnecessary appendage to the true function of the Golden Cascade. She found what she wanted, a writing pad on the bar counter and she took it back to the foyer. There, at a table by a potted palm, she scribbled a hasty note to Harvey. "I'm shortly going to Falmouth. Could I see you first?" and signed it 'K.T.' She folded it in two and beckoned to one of the page-boys. He came reluctantly, whistling a few bars from—'She's only a bird in a gilded cage.' She ignored his impudence and told him to deliver the note to a Mr Stephens at the Queen's Hotel and wait for an answer.

He was back within ten minutes. The gentleman had booked out that morning and left no forwarding address, So that was that—it was meant to be. She went slowly up the stairs her delight in an unexpected holiday eclipsed by her disappointment.

She decided to go to Falmouth the following Wednesday, giving Maggie two clear days in her new home before descending on her. Vi came to Paddington to see her off.

"I've lost count of the number of times I've done this," she complained. She wasn't grumbling; she was glad Kitty was having this chance to be with her family again, but she was going to miss her. The gilt was beginning to peel from the Golden Cascade as far as she was concerned, and she wished she could escape from it too, even for a few days.

Kitty had chosen a severe tailor-made dress in grey flannel to travel in, one that she had bought herself, and with it she wore a small astrakhan hat with muff to match. They found a 'Ladies Only' compartment vacant and Vi sat down with her until the train was due out.

"We haven't had much time to talk these last few days," Vi hesitated, then plunged on. "You never did tell me what happened that night you wore the emeralds. Something did, I know—you've been as edgy as a knife ever since and all sorts of rumours are going the rounds—."

"I can well imagine," said Kitty drily.

"You won't bite my head off if I ask if it's anything to do with Harvey?"

Kitty smiled weakly. "No, I won't bite your head off, Vi—I know I've been impossible to live with lately, and I'm sorry." She shifted her gaze to the window, watching the passengers converging on the platform. "You know of course that Harvey came to the casino?"

"I know somebody came and there was a bit of hanky-panky at one of the tables. You know I saw Harvey."

Kitty looked round swiftly. "When?"

"That night. You'd gone to sleep and I had a right old headache. I was cooling it on the winder, looking out—thinking like, when I saw this bloke in the room opposite. He was standing so still he give me the creeps. He looked kind of—" Vi paused, groping for the right word, "haunted, you might say. You said you'd seen Harvey and I wouldn't believe you. You were right about something else. The Golden Cascade is nothing but a 'igh-class knocking-house—it come home to me that night. What sort of turns do it get? The likes of Marie Lloyd and Dan Leno wouldn't touch it with a ten-foot barge pole. The music-hall part is only a sham, hiding what really goes on. Anyway, girl, you'll be out of it for a month. Good luck to you."

Vi rose. Two elderly ladies accompanied by a porter with their luggage were making a crotchety entrance. "Goodbye Kitty, don't do what I wouldn't do." She planted a hasty kiss on Kitty's cheek and jumped down. Kitty leaned out of the window to wave goodbye. In her emerald-green and white striped gown Vi stood out on the platform like a cockatoo among sparrows.

Kitty passed the journey as far as Swindon flicking through two periodicals Vi had bought at the station book-stall. *Tit-Bits*, and a new magazine—*Pearson's Weekly*. But she couldn't keep her mind on the printed page; superimposed images, chiefly of Harvey, displaced her thoughts. It was a relief when a steward announced that luncheon was being served.

While she waited for her order Kitty glanced fleetingly round the first-class restaurant car. Bruno was paying her expenses so she was travelling in style. Only half the tables were occupied, it was not yet one o'clock. With a shock of surprise she saw that one of the diners was Harvey, sitting with his back to her halfway down the coach. A thought came to her that somehow he had discovered she was going to Falmouth and had joined the train on purpose to meet her, but that idea soon faded when she saw his companion.

She was a handsome woman, fashionably plump, richly dressed in figured silk with dolman sleeves and lace cuffs. Her hat was a feathered toque in honey-brown, so similar in colour to her plentiful hair that from a distance it looked like an elaborate extension of her hair-style. She had large eyes which she rolled constantly as she talked, and she used her hands emphatically to make a point. Her hands were very white, dimpled at the knuckles. Her complexion was the colour of cream. Kitty dipped her spoon into her soup so viciously some slopped over and stained the starched cloth.

The pair had reached the coffee stage. Harvey lit a slim cigar. His companion produced cigarettes from her bag and inserted one into a holder, bending forward for Harvey to light it, her eyes gleaming with mischief. Obviously she realized she was causing a mild sensation by smoking in public. It was unusual for a lady to do so.

To Kitty's embarrassment they came in her direction to leave the dining-car. She lifted the menu up to her face, but Harvey had already noticed her. It was obvious he had been taken by surprise at her presence, and she got some satisfaction from seeing him redden. He bowed and his companion stared at her with frank curiosity. She walked in a cloud of perfume, her skirt trailing on the carpeted floor, the bows and lace on her well-decorated bustle swaying with each step. "Such ostentation," Kitty overheard from the next table. A plain woman was glaring after them. "An American, naturally!" as if it were some sort of disease.

Kitty saw them again at Plymouth. There was a lengthy wait here and some of the passengers alighted in order to stretch their legs while the guard van was loaded and unloaded. Gazing idly out of the window Kitty saw Harvey and the woman coming along the platform, a porter following behind pushing a barrow holding a large trunk. The woman walked with a graceful swaying movement, just her finger-tips resting on the crook of Harvey's arm. They didn't see her, they were too engrossed in each other, the woman still talking, still gesticulating.

Soon after leaving Plymouth the train rattled over the Royal Albert Bridge at Saltash and Kitty felt an uplift of her heart as she always did when reaching Cornwall. She recalled a previous journey when an old countryman from north Cornwall had pointed out the naval ships moored at Devonport and then nodded to the bridge. "I can remember that bridge being built thirty year ago, Brunel just lived to see it hisself afore he died. It linked Cornwall with the rest of England and let in all those foreigners from up-along." Was that what she was now in her latest London fashions—a 'foreigner from up-along'?

The ever-faithful Dave was there to meet her at Falmouth, and to his embarrassment she flung her arms round him, she was so pleased to see him. She had never shown such fervour towards him before, and he wasn't to know that in her present state of mind he stood for all that was dependable and unchanging.

Outside the station stood a pony and trap. "Dave—what extravagance!" then she remembered the distance to the new house. She enjoyed the drive. The air was always so exhilarating after the pollution of the capital. She loved to see the lights in the rigging of ships at anchor and fancied they were stars bobbing a welcome. The gentle night breeze caressed her cheek like a friendly kiss. Yes, this was home.

"You don't know how lucky you are to live here, Dave. You can't imagine what it's like in London. Smelly, sooty, dirty."

"I'm not sure I need to imagine it," said Dave gravely. "I had my share of bad air in the mines."

"Were you glad to leave?"

"Dear God yes, I couldn't have stuck it much longer. But it's all thanks to you, Kitty, for keeping us going until the fishing trade picked up again. We owe you so much."

Tears pricked her eyes. Perhaps she did owe a debt to the Golden Cascade after all, Dave's simple gratitude made many things worth while. She enquired after Maggie.

"She's well enough, considering. Like a cat with two tails over the new house, though I hope she hasn't made you expect anything too grand. It's not up to your old home in Laburnum Road, and we haven't much in the way of furniture yet, though we're getting your father's out of store."

"How is Father?"

"Oh, he's a lot better, especially now—" Dave stopped, then cleared his throat as if he were gaining time to think what to say next. "I wasn't going to mention this quite so soon, was going to give you a chance to get home first, but there's a boat-yard just come on the market over Penlith way and your father is there now, talking business with the previous owner. I'm joining them later—"

"But Dave, he'll need capital. Look what happened when he was in business before—it was a disaster."

"Times have changed Kitty, there's a call for pleasure craft now, and steam ferries. Summer visitors want to go sightseeing, and ther's a lot to be seen up the different creeks. Only boats can get to some places. The future's wide open—"

"That doesn't sound like you talking, Dave."

Dave went quiet as if he had been reprimanded and no matter how hard she tried Kitty couldn't get him back on the subject. The news was good that her father was at last showing some initiative; why then did she have this feeling of unease?

They turned into a road of small pleasant bow-windowed villas. Maggie had heard the sound of the trap and was at the door to meet them. Light from the hall illuminated the small front garden. Except for a slight thickening of the waist Maggie looked the same as ever, her broad face wreathed with smiles.

"Let me look at you," she said, holding Kitty out at arm's length. "My, you look pretty, but you're too thin—much too thin. We must try and fatten you up while we've got you."

"Where's Joe?"

"Where else at this time of night? Fast asleep in his cot. Go up and see him then come down and have your supper."

There was no gas connected upstairs. Maggie had given Kitty a candle and by the light of this she looked down with unappeased hunger at her small son. He was sleeping on his stomach with his auburn head twisted to one side. The lashes that curved on his flushed cheek were gold-specked like Harvey's and in the shape of his brow and line of his chin she could also trace his father's features. She couldn't tear herself away from him, devouring him with her eyes, until Maggie came up for her, saying supper would be spoiled.

Kitty was hungry, she had hardly touched her meal on the train, and Maggie's baked mackerel was an old favourite. Afterwards, she was given a conducted tour of the house. Maggie, bubbling over with pride at her new possession, though trying to appear unheeding. "But wait until you see what we didn't even have at Laburnum Road," she said with satisfaction.

It turned out to be a bath with a cold water tap and a plug to let the water out after use. Not in a room of its own, that would be expecting too much even for seven-and-six a week, but in the scullery. Kitty hadn't noticed it at first because it was hidden under a wooden cover, but when Maggie lifted this there it was in all its pristine newness. Kitty imagined Maggie polishing it every day.

"I bet you won't allow Dave or Father to use it," she laughed. "I bet they'll still have to bath in the old tin tub in front of the kitchen fire."

"Don't be silly, Kitty, of course they won't. Look, the copper is right here. I'll just have to heat the water in that then ladle it into the bath and cold water's laid on. No more baling the dirty bath-water out into buckets; do you remember? Dave's going to cover the lid with oil-cloth for me, and it'll make a handy table when we're not using it as a bath."

Because the kitchen was the only room completely furnished, they sat there for the rest of the evening. Maggie pulled two easy chairs up to the fire. "Come on, put your feet on the fender, and we'll have a real heart-to-heart. There won't be any interruptions. Dave's gone to return the trap and then he's off on some errand or other."

Kitty looked reproachfully at her sister. "You know he's gone to Penlith—he told me about it. Has Harvey anything to do with it?"

Maggie looked uncomfortable. "Harvey? What made

you think of Harvey?"

"Because I saw him only a few days ago; he came to the Cascade. Why didn't you warn me?"

Maggie poked the fire. It didn't need it but she had to give vent to her feelings somehow. "I'm tired of you two—why can't you be honest with each other? *He* mustn't know about Joe. *You* mustn't know he is back in England—"

"How long has he been back?"

"Some time I believe. You know Father wrote to him when Adrian died."

Kitty started. "*Father.*"

"Yes, I think he felt it was up to him to put things right between you once more. Don't laugh, he addressed the letter to Harvey, care of the gold fields, out-back, Australia—and it got to him eventually." Maggie looked sideways at her sister. "How did Harvey seem? He said he wanted to surprise you."

"He did that all right," said Kitty, flaring up. "He made quite an entrance. Wanted to surprise me—that's rich." Remembering the ugly scene in her room a wave of bitterness went over her. "What about that Americam woman. Who is she?"

Maggie looked up. "I know nothing about an American woman."

"It so happened that Harvey caught my train as far as Plymouth, and she was with him. I think she's American, very well-dressed, wealthy too, I should say. It did cross my mind she might be his wife. She was wearing a wedding ring."

"Oh Kitty, you do sound sour." Maggie sighed; this wasn't the homecoming she'd envisaged, the cosy sisterly chat. She had wanted to discuss her house, ask Kitty's advice about wall-papers and curtains. Thinking about the house her mind branched off into another direction. "You'd better know that Harvey may be settling down in

Falmouth. He's interested in his old home. It's on the market again."

Kitty had a mental picture of the Stephens' property perched on its hill, with sloping lawns and wide terraces. "A bachelor would rattle in a place like that!" She got to her feet, scraping her chair on the lino. "I'm sorry, Maggie, I must go up, I'm too tired to wait for the men. Say good-night to them for me."

But tired though she was, sleep was a long time coming. She tried not to toss about too much in case of waking Joe. Finally, long after she heard Dave locking up, she drifted into a fitful sleep, but even then her dreams were haunted by the spectre of a woman with honey-brown hair.

FOURTEEN

It took Kitty just over a week to gain little Joe's complete trust. His premature birth and a prolonged illness before he was a year old had retarded his growth, made hin more babyish than his years. He was also backward in talking, but alert enough. His wide dark eyes missed nothing.

He would cling to Maggie, peeping round her skirts at Kitty, ready to duck out of sight if she made any attempt to approach. One day she coaxed a smile from him. She tried bribery, holding out a sugar stick to bring him to her. He soon began to equate her with pleasant things like sweets and presents.

Maggie did all she could to foster their growing relationship. She had never been a usurper herself, and showed no jealousy at Kitty's attempts to win Joe away from her. It was at her suggestion that Kitty began to take

Joe for a daily walk, pushing him in a three-wheeled baby-carriage that Dave had bought secondhand, and it was during these spells together that the bond between mother and child was finally sealed.

One day her father accompanied them. They walked as far as the old town and sat to rest on the quayside. Joe had fallen asleep, his head drooping forward, his chin buried in his chest. When Kitty tried to push him back on to the pillow, her father stopped her. "Let him be. Children of that age are like young puppies, they can sleep curled up in a ball. It won't hurt him."

They sat in companionable silence, looking out over a scene that never ceased to delight them. Then her father began to tell her about the Penlith boatyard. She realized that the very idea had given him a new lease of life. She said something about hoping it would be a success. "Of course it'll be a success. You don't think Harvey would risk his capital otherwise, do you? Neither Dave nor I have any money to put into it. All we've got to offer is our experience of boats and knowing the seas around here like the backs of our hands."

She had guessed, ever since hearing of the new venture, that it must be Harvey who was putting up the capital. And yet he had been willing to risk it at the gaming-tables. There was so much she couldn't understand.

"Is Harvey very rich?"

"That depends on what you call rich. I'd say more like he was just comfortable—"

"But all that gold!"

He gave her one of his slow smiles that rolled away the years, and she was a small girl again who had just said something outrageous but amusing. "All what gold? Some nuggets panned out of creeks and surface reefs, that's all. The real mining was going on further outback. Harvey was going off there when he got my letter and decided to come home instead. He came home for you, Kitty."

If only she could believe that. Tears came readily to her eyes. How could she shatter the hopes of this simple man. He went on in his benign way gazing dreamily out at sea. "The boatyard is really for you. He's making Dave and me partners, but its for you—for the old days, when he first came to work for me, and you were a child clambering about the yard. He's trying to put the clock back, we know."

Because she made no response he looked round, and saw a single tear rolling down her cheek. He put one horny, work-worn hand over both hers. "Oh child, if only you had waited instead of rushing off to marry that London chap. But there, I mustn't say that. We wouldn't have had little Joe, would we? We wouldn't have had our little Joe."

She felt she couldn't take anymore. She got to her feet, helped her father to his. "Come along there's a mist coming up from the sea, and we'll get chilled if we sit any longer." She walked ahead all the way home so that her father couldn't see her face.

But she was given compensation that evening. She was singing Joe to sleep after bathing him. Maggie downstairs, stitching a bodice for the coming baby, put her head on one side to listen. It was years since she had heard Kitty sing, and she recognized the song Dave had taught them long ago.

"Here's health to the Pope, may he live to repent,
And add half a year to the time of his Lent,
To teach all his children from Rome to the Poles,
There's nothing like pilchards for saving their souls."

Maggie wasn't the only one to be delighted. Little Joe held his arms out to Kitty. "More Mummy-Two," he chortled. "More song."

Mummy-Two! It didn't matter that she had been relegated to second place—he had called her Mummy. She kissed him until he squealed.

The next day was bright but with a stiff breeze. Maggie wrapped Joe in one of her own woollen shawls and tied it in a bunch at the back. She was always fearful of him catching a chill. Kitty had to borrow something from Maggie too as she had brought nothing with her suitable for beach wear. She was wearing a serge skirt much too big for her, a velveteen jacket going thin at the elbows and a plush tam-o'-shanter. She didn't care how she looked, since being called Mummy-Two life for her had taken on a new dimension. They were off to the beach to play Joe's favourite game—ducks and drakes.

The three-wheeled rickety carriage was difficult enough to steer on the pavement, on the sand it was impossible. Joe got out and walked. From behind he looked like a walking bundle of wool. Kitty laughed aloud. Looking around, the meaning of Dave's words— 'The future is wide open'—came home to her. Even though October was approaching, there were still visitors occupying the glass shelters along the promenade, and a very superior hotel was in the process of being erected. Did Falmouth have a future as a holiday resort? The prospects seemed promising.

They stood at the seas' edge skimming stones along the surface of the water. Dave had taught Kitty the knack when she hadn't been much older than Joe. Joe was happy to throw his stones in with a loud 'plonk', screaming with excitement each time one hit the water. An incoming wave caught them unawares, and Kitty snatched Joe up in time to save them both from a wetting. He put his arms round her neck and kissed her, the first time he had ever done so voluntarily, and she responded by hugging him close to her, nuzzling his cheek with hers.

And it was standing like that, outlined against the sky, the wind whipping up her skirts that Harvey came upon her. She had seen someone approaching, but had been looking into the setting sun and was too dazzled to recognize him. When he was near enough he raised his hat. He was wearing a tweed coat with cape attached and looked like a prosperous country gentleman. She was devastated to think she had been caught in such shabby clothes, and with little Joe cocooned in such a ridiculous shawl.

It was hard to tell from Harvey's expression what he was thinking. He looked as nonplussed as herself. She suffered agonies thinking he was comparing her with his stylish American friend—or wife? She compressed her lips in a tight line, not responding to his faint smile of welcome. He looked at Joe thoughtfully, and again she felt outrage that he should catch him looking so outlandish.

Joe grew restless and she let him slide out of her arms. He ran off to get his bucket. Harvey looked at her with sober eyes. "Maggie told me where to find you. I wanted to talk to you." She inclined her head and fell in step beside him. They walked to the nearest shelter where she had left the pram, and sat down, facing the sea. Joe was squatting on his haunches filling his bucket with shells.

She waited for Harvey to break the silence, but he seemed ill-at-ease, tracing patterns in the blown sand with his stick. Then he looked up and watched Joe. "He's a fine boy."

"He needs building up."

"He'll soon catch up. I was very puny myself at that age. Or so my nurse told me, I don't remember of course." He went back to tracing patterns. Why was he making this stilted conversation? He was the one who had wanted to talk. Had he nothing to say about his behaviour at the Golden Cascade, or their encounter on the train? Had it been so unimportant to him that he had already

171

forgotten? Her pride came up like a barrier.

The sun was sinking rapidly, a round livid ball in an opaque sky. When she turned from watching it she saw Harvey studying her. He looked away. "Why did you cut your hair?" She told him of her illness but not the reason for it. "It's a pity. You had beautiful hair."

Adrian had found it beautiful too. It had fascinated him. He had liked nothing better than to unpin it and play with it; to brush it and strand it, and pile it up on her head to see the effect. Sometimes he would take up handfuls and bury his face in it, and then begin to kiss it. She had found his behaviour distasteful though she submitted dutifully, seeing it as another form of his sensuality. Both Maggie and Vi had on occasions urged her to grow her hair again. One of the reasons she wouldn't was because of Adrian. She kept it short to spite him—her antagonism towards him reaching out beyond the grave. I'm not a nice person, she thought, I bear grudges. She felt a grudge towards Harvey now because he spoke of light matters when there were much deeper issues at stake, and even as she was forming that thought in her mind, he said; "I wanted to apologize for my behaviour at our last meeting."

Our last meeting? He was ignoring the chance encounter on the train or had no wish to refer to it. She felt her inside gather together in a knot of anger. "I'd rather not discuss it."

"I acted like a cad. I don't know what came over me. Well, I do really, but I don't think you want me to dwell on that," with a glance at her tight lips. Yet, he blundered on; "I was in a reckless mood—I wanted to show off too. Then I saw your emeralds and realized I couldn't compete with those—"

She grew more tense. "You still believe—"

"No—no. I put that badly. But I saw him in your bedroom, as I thought. I saw him bending over you in a

172

very intimate fashion—I suppose I was jealous, though I know I have no claim on you, not any more. We have both gone our separate ways."

"Yes." She said bleakly, her anger being replaced by a feeling of desolation. Their paths had diverged and the distance would widen; they had lost their precious gift of communication when a glance—a touch of the hand—had been more potent than words. "But there is one last thing I want to say. I never was and never will be Bruno Chalk's mistress. I am paid very handsomely for my services; perhaps you don't approve of them, but they have stood me in very good stead these past few years."

He cleared his throat. "That's what I wanted to bring up. I admit I did disapprove of the Golden Cascade, I couldn't see why you didn't stay in Falmouth and find paid work here. But I realize now that wouldn't have been practical. Your family relied on you, they needed every penny you sent them from London just to survive. I can only guess at the sacrifices you've had to make—"

She stopped him with an impatient gesture. "I see Maggie's been talking—"

"No. Not Maggie—your father, actually."

"Oh, my father." She had an insane urge to laugh though she had never felt less like laughing. "So he made you feel ashamed of yourself. He packed you off to apologize."

"Don't be bitter, Kitty. I already felt very ashamed. I would have come to make my peace before but I only got back from London late last night—"

"And saw my father at Penlith this morning and had a nice little discussion about me. Thank you." She got quickly to her feet and called to Joe. Harvey rose also, towering above her.

"It's so difficult to talk to you. You snap back at me, everything I say."

"It was you suggested this talk, not me." Even now, if

he would only say he loved her, make some reference to their past, she would go gladly into his arms. But he stood with head lowered, his expression taut, and the shadow of the woman on the train stood behind him.

Little Joe came trotting up swinging his bucket. He held an empty mussel shell which he offered to Harvey. "Look boat," he said. "Likkle boat."

Kitty heard Harvey's sharp intake of breath. He bent and caught hold of the boy swinging him above his head before putting him down again. "You grand little chap. You remembered—yes, boat."

Kitty picked Joe up and despite his protests strapped him in the baby carriage. "What did you mean about him remembering?"

"Oh, didn't you know—before you returned to Falmouth, when we were still negotiating for the yard at Penlith, Dave would bring Joe along some afternoons to give Miggie a chance to rest. I needed Dave's opinion on some of the existing stock-in-trade. I taught Joe how to float mussel shells in a bucket of water. We became great pals, didn't we, Boy?"

The old pet name for Joe falling so familiarly from Harvey's lips was like a double blow. She had to get away at once, now, before her feelings revealed themselves.

The baby-carriage jarred on the pavement, the single front wheel catching in a rut. "Here, let me help you," said Harvey. "You can't push that thing, it's not stable."

"I can manage, thank you. I don't need help." She could tell that he was hoping to be asked back to the house. She said a formal goodbye and walked off swiftly, only looking back when she had to cross the road. He still stood there, a lone figure, leaning on his stick watching her out of sight.

Maggie was preparing mutton chops for supper and hardly glanced up, though she did comment on their healthy colour. Kitty gave Joe his tea, undressed him and got him ready for bed. He lay on his side, sucking his thumb, watching her as she floated a night-light in a saucer of water and put a match to it. She bent over the cot and brushed a strand of bright hair out of his eyes. "Say night-night, Mummy-Two. Say Mummy-Two again," she pleaded, but he would not, punishing her for having not sung to him. Just like his father, she thought, going downstairs.

Maggie looked round with a smile as she entered the kitchen. "He's gone off, then—he's no trouble, is he?" Her smile faded. "What's the matter, Kitty?"

"Why did Dave take Joe over to Penlith, to the boat-yard when Harvey was there?"

Maggie stared. "Why not?"

"You know why not. Dangling Joe in front of Harvey like a carrot."

Maggie gasped, and sat down rather suddenly. "What a thing to say. Dangling Joe about like a carrot—what do you mean?"

"You know what I mean—flaunting Joe like that, hoping Harvey would tumble to the fact that he was his own son—"

"Kitty! What's come over you. Fancy thinking such a thing—you're a devil. My Dave—do you really believe his mind works like that? He's a simple man—a kind man. He always took Joe out on his day off to give me a break, until you came and took over." Maggie broke down and began to cry, putting her head into her arms, and Kitty stared at her in a stupid fasion, holding back her own tears with difficulty.

"Maggie don't—don't cry like that. You never cry—"

"You're enough to make anyone cry. Always ready to fly off the handle—I don't know where I am with you, sometimes."

Kitty went to her, putting an arm across her shoulders. "Do you remember what you used to say to me when I was expecting—that if I cried I'd have a fretful baby? Maggie dear, please don't. I'm sorry—I didn't mean it—it's just—well, I met Harvey again, and it's awful. It's just as if we're strangers."

Maggie grew calm, sniffed, then blew her nose on a man's-size handkerchief. She looked up at Kitty and the glazed, hurt look in her eyes slowly diffused. "Put the kettle on. We'll have a cup of tea—the chops can wait."

Over tea, Kitty told of the meeting on the beach. "He said he wanted to talk to me. I thought now—it's either to tell me he's married or else perhaps to suggest, to ask, well, you know—to try and get back to our old relationship. But he didn't. He went very quiet. He seemed so preoccupied—lost in himself. He didn't even mention that woman!"

"Perhaps you're making too much of that. And you're not always easy to talk to, Kitty."

"I know. I fly off the handle—you just said." Kitty sighed, staring blankly into her untouched cup of tea. "Oh Maggie, I wish I could explain, but sometimes I just go all tight inside, and the things I really want to say won't come out." It was Maggie's turn to comfort Kitty. They smiled feebly at each other. "Aren't we a fine pair?" said Maggie. "Sitting here watering our tea. Slip into the scullery and rinse your face and for goodness sake change out of that awful skirt. And I'd better get these chops in the pan or there'll be no supper ready for the men."

Kitty went back to Gyllingvase beach the following day, and the day after, hoping for another meeting with Harvey and determined to show a willingness to be friends at least. Then she heard from her father that he had gone to London to arrange a short-term loan until the rest of his capital could be transferred from Australia. The next day came a telegram from Vi. It read; "Come back at once. All hell is let loose."

Maggie was shocked at such a word being allowed for

anyone in the postal service to see, but Kitty was amused, wondering if the telegraph clerk had had to add the aitch. That was one word Vi never aspirated, either speaking or writing. She didn't take the summons seriously, knowing Vi. No doubt a row had blown up between her and one of the other girls, or even with Bruno himself.

Then one evening Harvey appeared. They had had supper and were sitting in the parlour. Maggie had lit a fire and only the day before, the sofa and easy chairs from Laburnum Road had been brought out of store. Kitty had picked some sprays of fuchsia still blooming on the heights above Killigrew Street, and she was drowsy from the heat of the fire, her eyes fixed on the red and purple flowers which in her mind stood as a symbol for Cornwall, when the knock came. Instinctively she knew it was Harvey and she thought—this might be my last chance—I mustn't waste it.

Harvey came into the room blinking in the light. He was dressed in a tweed ulster and carried one of the hats which had recently come into fashion and were known as Trilbys. Maggie at once jumped up, welcoming and solicitous. "Have you had supper? Can I make you a cup of tea? I'm afraid we haven't anything stronger."

He smilingly explained that he had eaten on the train. He had come on from Truro where he was staying. "I can't stop long, I'm afraid, I must catch the next train back. I have an early appointment with an architect in the morning, and then my solicitor." He addressed them all, but he looked at Kitty. He drew a newspaper from his pocket and spread it out on the sofa-table. It was a late edition of the London Evening News which he had bought to read on the train. He pointed to a headline, which to Kitty seemed to leap out of the paper and hit her like a blow.

BARONET COMMITS SUICIDE IN A MAYFAIR CASINO.

She read and re-read the following paragraphs with a sense of unreality. A Captain Sir Walter Appley had booked one of the private rooms in the Golden Cascade and then shot himself through the head with his own revolver. At the inquest it was revealed that he had gaming debts of ten thousand pounds. The Golden Cascade had been closed by order of the Home Office and the owner was being deported as an undesirable alien.

"Well, I never!" said Maggie when other exclamations had ceased. "All I can say is, Kitty, that it's a mercy you're here and not there in the midst of it. What a pretty kettle of fish!"

"I'm going back—I must," said Kitty vehemently. "It's not only Bruno. It's Vi—the other girls—my place is with them."

But Maggie and Dave protested at this outburst. Maggie volubly, Dave in his slow grave manner. Joseph Tredennick surprised them by saying; "I think Kitty must do the honourable thing. Go back and work out her notice and then come back here for good."

Kitty stared. All this time, had her father thought of her as a waitress in some superior restaurant? She caught Harvey's eye and quickly looked away, detecting a gleam of amusement. In spite of herself her lips twitched. "I'm going back," she said. "I must."

Harvey shook hands with them all. He had to leave. Was it wishful thinking on her part that he gave hers an extra squeeze? "You're a brave girl," he said, too low for the others to hear. "I admire you."

Later she went to the kitchen to put on the kettle for their evening cocoa. Maggie joined her wearing a look of smug satisfaction. "Well, what do you think of that?" she said, putting bricks into the oven to warm.

"I think it's a tragedy," said Kitty. "You don't realize how many people will be affected by it."

Maggie looked perplexed, then her face cleared. "Oh that—the Golden Cascade—I'm not going to waste any thought on that! I'm talking about Harvey. Why do you think he came all the way out from Truro tonight? To save you from hearing about it from anyone else. He wanted to warn you. That shows you how much he still cares."

"I hadn't thought of that," said Kitty slowly.

"There's a lot you haven't thought about, and there's a lot more you'll have to face up to. When are you going to tell Harvey the truth about Joe?"

Kitty gave her sister a long steady look. "When I come back again. I promise you that, Maggie."

She went up to bed before the others as she had to make an early start in the morning. She put the hot brick wrapped in its piece of protective flannel into the bed to warm it while she undressed. There was no need to light a candle, she could see well enough by night-light. She bent over the cot to kiss Joe. The last three mornings he had awakened first, banging the sides of his cot, one impatient leg thrust out between the bars. "Out Mummy-Two—out," he had demanded. Would he miss her? Would he cry for her? She thought he might. With her finger-tip she gently traced the outline of his cheek, the curve of his mouth, the dimple at the side of his chin. This beautiful, cherished child would be waiting for her—and for Harvey.

FIFTEEN

She alighted from the cab at the door of the Golden
Cascade late the following afternoon. When she rang,
Withers the doorman let her in. He was not in uniform.
He looked tired and when she asked him how things were
he shook his head dolefully. Inside all was quiet. No
preparatory evening rush—-no scurrying page-boys—no
attentive waiters—no music—no flowers—just a
funereal hush.

Vi wasn't in their apartment and all her clothes were
gone from the wardrobe. Kitty removed her outer gar-
ments and flung them on the bed. She sprinkled eau-de-
cologne on the palms of her hands and dabbed her cheeks
and forehead with it. Refreshed, she felt ready to face
Bruno.

He was sprawled in his usual chair in the office,

smoking a cigar with a half-empty decanter of whisky at his elbow. His eyes were puffy and red-rimmed, otherwise he looked much the same. She had expected some change. Despair perhaps, or a sense of defeat. But he greeted her with a sardonic smile.

"So—the lamb has come back to the fold. Isn't she frightened of the big bad wolf?"

Kitty ignored this. "Where's everybody?"

"Some went of their own accord. Some went reluctantly—some needed a helpful push—"

"I bet you had to push Vi."

"Indeed I did, but I can't say it was out of any concern for me. She wanted to wait for your return. She left a message—you'll find her with a certain Ma Watling. Charming name—it conjures up a vision of sheer delight."

She decided it was the whisky talking. "I came back to see if there is anything I can do to help."

"What a magnanimous gesture. Such as?"

She came forward, leaning on the desk with her hands, facing him. "Don't laugh at me. You've been so good to me. Isn't there anything I can do?"

"Would you marry me?"

She drew back. "You know I wouldn't. I don't love you."

He let out a bellow of laughter. "Oh Kitty, you are priceless. Did you consider love when you married your unfortunate husband? Don't worry, dear, I wasn't serious, I'm not interested in marriage—it's too permanent." He squinted at her through his cigar-smoke. "All the same, we'd make a good pair, you and I. Come away with me."

"Bruno, be serious. What's going to happen to you now?"

"Well, I'm being booted out of this country for a start. I could put up a fight—I'm not an alien as the popular press insists on calling me; I'm actually a Canadian, but there's nothing to keep me here now. I've lost everything. I may as well try and make another start somewhere else."

She looked at him, frowning. "But you'll be able to sell the Cascade. That should give you enough to live on in comfort."

"Depends on the meaning of the word comfort, my dear. But as it happens, I can't sell this place. It's mortgaged up to the hilt—and so by the way, is the Silver Cascade. I'm a gambler too, you know. Not at the tables, but on the stock-exchange, and I didn't have an attractive young lady giving a nod to my broker in the nick of time," he added in a self-mocking manner.

"Do you mean to say you are *ruined?*"

"There again, it depends on the meaning of the word ruined. I think I can scrape up enough to see me to San Francisco. With these I could raise enough to open a trim little saloon on the Barbary Coast. What do you think?" While he had been talking he had opened his desk, and now dangled the emerald necklace before her. It slipped through his fingers like green fire, an illusion of wealth, a bait for the alarm that surged through her.

"Bruno—you told me they didn't belong to you—that they were only on loan."

He dropped them back into the drawer, turned the key. "So they are—and back they go tomorrow. They had to be repaired—remember?" He laughed quietly. "What a law-abiding little creature you are at heart—how you must have hated the casino. Come, be honest with me. You did?"

She nodded, too miserable to look up. "Well, you need worry no longer. From now on this place will become a respectable music-hall, if that isn't a contradiction of terms, and will attract such performers as Marie Lloyd, Lottie Collins, Vesta Tilley—Dan Leno. Oh yes, it will quite rival the Oxford. And what about you? What will you do?"

"I shall be all right. I have some money saved—"

"You have money saved." He was mocking her now. "May I enquire how much?"

"Nearly two hundred pounds."

"Nearly *two* hundred pounds!" He made a face of exaggerated astonishment. "What a thrifty little soul—I didn't know I was harbouring a financial genius." Suddenly all the bounce left him. He stubbed out his cigar and came over to Kitty, taking her by her shoulders. "I meant it, you know, about coming away with me. I love you, Kitty. I wouldn't give a damn about losing all this if I could keep you. Damn you, don't look at me like that." Without warning he took hold of her and pressed his warm wet lips against her own, and instinctively she fought back, pressing the heels of her palms against his shoulders. He let her go and she stepped back out of reach, wiping her mouth with the back of her hand.

"Am I so objectionable?" he said bitterly.

"Oh, don't think that—it isn't that. I can't help it. I hate being kissed."

"Except by Harvey Stephens." He shrugged. "I should have guessed. There'll never be anybody else for you, will there? Well, at least let us part without bitterness. Will you shake hands?"

His hand was moist and hot like his mouth; she withdrew her own quickly. "I do wish you all success for the future. I do hope you make that fresh start."

He gave a wry smile. "Don't you worry about me. This won't be the first time I've lost a fortune and found it again. I like nothing better than a challenge—it puts me on my mettle." But at the back of his eyes was a look of affliction. He knew time was running out; each fresh start took its toll.

She turned round at the door to raise her hand in a last salute, but he had his back to her, his shoulders sagging, a broken man. She blinked back tears as she went to her room.

She packed her case taking only clothes she had bought with her own money. She said goodbye to Withers and slipped some sovereigns into his hand. As the cab pulled away she looked out of the window at her last sight of the Golden Cascade. At a first floor window a curtain moved. Bruno was saying goodbye too.

Returning to the little house in Nelson Street was like putting the clock back two years. Vi's hair was a burnished red, she wore a scarlet dress ornamented with gold frogging. Ma was pedalling away at a new treadle-machine. The only changes were for the better—new furniture—new curtains—a Turkey rug by the fireplace. "It's good to see you again, girl," said Vi, hugging her. Kitty could have been away three years instead of weeks on the strength of their welcome. "Come on, sit 'ere by the fire, and I'll pop down to Angel Lane and get some haddocks."

"No, I'm not hungry," protested Kitty, laughing. "I just want to know about you two. How are you getting on?"

"I'm fine. I'm back at the Silver Cascade—their star turn—no joking. The new management wanted me back; with all that talk in the papers the customers have been queueing up to see me." Vi gave one of her outrageous laughs, and for all her exaggeration Kitty knew there was a lot of truth in what she said. "What about you, girl? Been to the Golden Cascade yet?"

Kitty glossed over her leave-taking with Bruno. "Poor little devil," said Vi, gazing into the fire. "I couldn't 'elp feeling sorry for him." Her mood veered again. "But I must say for me own sake, I'm glad to be back in Stratford again."

"What about the tea-shop?" Kitty teased. "You haven't given up your dream of that."

Vi gave another laugh. "Can you really see me in a black gown an' a white apron talking all posh-like to me customers? Anyway 'oo drinks tea—women! Give me men for company any time. What I'd really like is a nice pub." Her tawny eyes went dreamy. "A public like 'The Two Puddings'—that would just about suit us, wouldn't it, Ma?"

Kitty waited impatiently to hear from Maggie, and received a letter in a matter of days. She mentioned Harvey but only in reference to the boatyard, where the business transaction was now completed; and also that he had engaged an architect to plan modernization of the old family home. The rest of her letter was full of anecdotes of Joe, and how he kept asking for 'Mummy-Two'—"so don't keep him waiting too long," Maggie ended with. Kitty put the letter away with a light heart.

There was nothing now to keep her at Stratford, but she stayed on, scanning the paper daily, hoping for further news of Bruno. She couldn't return to Falmouth until her mind had been put at rest regarding him. Then one day a letter came from him containing a banker's draft for two hundred pounds. The letter was brief and without preamble;

"By the time you receive this I shall be on the high seas. Don't be too proud to accept the enclosed, it is only a small bonus and you are worth a lot more. While I was still a lad my father found a way to help me get what I wanted. Whatever I managed to save, he would double it. It was an encouragement I have never forgotten, and I would like to pass it on to you. I noticed you left your collection of gowns behind. What use do you think they would be to me? Please don't treat this money in the same way. Accept it in the spirit in which it is given, and if you have any doubts, ask your friend. Think of me sometimes—I won't go under, not yet."

"What does he mean?" asked Kitty, giving the letter to

Vi to read.

"It means, girl, that we were all given a farewell present—those that stood by 'im, I mean. Those that did a bunk didn't get a brass farthing. Wait here—"

Vi returned wearing a set of magnificent sable furs. She strutted about the room, displaying them for the benefit of Kitty and Ma. "How do I look—I feel like a bloomin' duchess. 'Ere I am, all dressed up and nowhere to go, ready to drop me aitches and pick 'em up again. Go on, have a feel, Kitty—it's just like silk."

Vi had exploded like a rocket when she discovered that Kitty had left her wardrobe behind at the Golden Cascade. "Thank the Lord we 'aven't all got your delicate feelings, else some of us wouldn't 'ave a stitch to our backs." Well, she has a very grand stitch to her back now, thought Kitty, amused.

There was one other thing to do before wrapping up her life in Stratford and storing it away in a mental drawer, and that was to say goodbye to her mother-in-law. She had kept in touch with Mrs Beatty, regularly sending her postal orders.

She had grown much thinner since Kitty had last seen her. The flesh had fallen away from her eyes leaving them even more protruding. "What's this for?" She looked at the banker's draft uncomprehendingly.

"It's for you—a going-away present. I'm leaving Stratford. I shan't be coming back, and I'd like you to have it, Mrs Beatty. I've checked with the bank and it is transferable. It was given to me, but I don't need the money. I want you to have it."

Mrs Beatty made no attempt to take the draft. It lay on the table between them—Kitty's indulgence. Her mother-in-law shook her head. "There's only one favour I really want. Go and see Adrian—you never have."

Her sister, who had kept tactfully out of their way, now came in with the tea-tray. Like her home, she gave out a

186

sense of warmth and friendliness. Afterwards, she saw Kitty to the door.

"She's slowly fading, you know. I don't think she really took it in about the money. It's such a big sum, I feel uncomfortable about it. She don't want for nothing—I see to that."

Kitty smiled assuringly, easing the other's embarrassment. "I can tell that. But don't worry about the money. I can spare it, honestly."

She visited the cemetery the next morning. Vi offered to go with her, but this was something she had to do on her own. She found the grave—opulent, in black marble with gilt lettering, just as Mrs Beatty had planned. By contrast the inscription was simple;

Adrian Beatty. 1855–1887.

R.I.P.

Standing in that lonely stillness with the fog turning to condensation on the trees and pattering all around in tiny droplets, Kitty felt a sense of peace steal over her. Her mother had been a wise person. She used to say—'Those whom we have wronged we hate the most'. She had wronged Adrian—she had used him—and out of her guilt had arisen hatred. But now that hatred had gone. There was nothing left—only a sense of relief. "Rest in Peace," she said. It was her valediction to Adrian.

This time Vi baulked at coming to Paddington with her. "I'm getting to hate the sight of that perishing station. We'll say our goodbyes 'ere—in private. I know I ain't going to see you again."

"You and Ma will always be welcome to come and stay."

"We'll see about that."

They held each other close, leaving Ma to do their weeping for them. Whether they would ever meet again was very much in the lap of the Gods. "Well, it only costs a penny to write," said Vi philosophically.

Fog still lingered in the narrow streets, muffling the sound of footfalls, the clip-clop of horses' hooves. Kitty had ordered a cab to take her all the way to Paddington. Ma was aghast at such extravagance. "It would only 'ave cost you tuppence on a tram!"

"Ah, but she's a lady of property now," said Vi, pleased to see Kitty spending money on herself for a change. Kitty had said nothing of her visit to Plaistowe.

She was sitting in the cab and the cabby was hoisting up her luggage when a postman loomed out of the murk. "Anyone 'ere know of a Mrs Beatty? I've got a letter for her, but no number on it."

"There's no-one of that name down this street," said Vi.

Kitty gave a start. "It's me," she said. "That's my name."

The postman snorted. "Well, next time, get whoever this is, to fill in the address properly. We 'ave enough walking to do without things being made more difficult for us." He walked away limping, he had a corn on his middle toe, and moisture was dripping off the back peak of his hat and trickling down his neck; it was one of those mornings.

" 'Appy soul," said Ma. But Vi had caught the expression on Kitty's face before she tucked the letter into her muff. "I reckon you think he's an angel of delight," she said, reaching up to give Kitty a last kiss. "Take care of yourself, girl, and don't forget to write."

Kitty had a compartment to herself for the first part of the journey. She had paid for a foot-warmer and had brought a lap-robe with her so she was comfortable and warm in her corner. She waited until the mean streets and dreary tenements had given way to leady suburbs before opening Harvey's letter. Her first sensation of felicity had now given way to doubt. Perhaps Harvey was writing to explain about the woman on the train. Perhaps she was his wife after all. Perhaps he was having his old home done over for her sake. Perhaps—perhaps—she thought, impatient with herself, perhapsing won't answer questions!

"My dearest," she read. Why had she worried? What but hope could follow that. "There are some things much easier to put on paper, and I'm going to take the easy way out. What I am going to say now, I wanted to say to you that day at Gyllingvase, but for reasons I'll come to later, I found I couldn't.

"I wish with all my heart I hadn't left you those years ago. I thought at the time I was doing the right thing, now I'm not so sure. I've made money certainly, not a lot, but enough. Could I have made a similar success at home, sticking it out through the hard times like Dave and your father and you? I wish I knew.

"I know now what I left you to. I was hurt and angry when I learnt that you had married Adrian Beatty. I couldn't understand how you could have got over me so quickly. I traced you to Stratford to ask you why—and saw you big with child. I thought the answer was simple. You had had to marry Adrian. I went off to Australia in such an ugly frame of mind, that even remembering now is like re-living some nightmare.

"Shall I tell you when the truth finally hit me, Kitty— my Kitty—That beautiful September day three weeks ago, when I came upon you at the beach with little Joe in your arms. You were wearing a bewitching little tam and looked so pretty. The sight of the two of you, your faces together, outlined by the sun has imprinted an image in my mind that will never fade. I knew at that moment who Joe's father was!

"I was so shaken by the revelation that had suddenly come to me that I dried up. I wanted to snatch you in my arms and kiss your dear face until you pleaded for mercy.

I wanted to crush you both with my love, but all I could do was to sit there like a dummy and hardly find a word to say for myself.

"So you married Adrian to give my son a name. Oh Kitty, what can I say? I've had it all out with Maggie. She says you didn't want me to know because you were fearful of being pitied. Oh my darling—pity! I'm the one to be pitied. I've lost you and I've lost my son—and the way I've acted towards you since I returned to England, how can I expect your forgiveness.

"You came to me so trustingly that day at Tregorra. You were so young and romantic and so wanted to believe that we were really married. I knew differently—but I couldn't resist you. I took advantage of you, that's the truth of it. My only excuse is that my love was too strong for me. My love for you is even stronger now. But now comes the delicate part. If I ask you to marry me will you believe it is out of pity, or because I feel Joe should have his rightful name, or any of that nonsense? I want you for my wife. I've always wanted you for my wife. There have been other woman—I'm no saint, but you're the only one I've ever loved. Could we pick up where we left off, Kitty? We are not the same people we were years ago—in some ways I think we have improved. We've both known un-happiness and a sense of loss. We've found each other again, and I believe found something just as important in the process—an awareness of each other's needs. That's not a bad basis for a marriage.

"Now I must come to something very prosaic. Maggie says you've been wondering about a woman you saw me with on the train. Good Lord, Kitty, I haven't given her a thought since that day. Do you remember my old college friend—the one who went to Pennsylvania and wrote asking me to join him? We could say, unfairly, that he was the one who parted us! Well, that was his wife come over here to visit her English cousins. She got in touch with me through my bank and when she learnt that I had business in Plymouth with a firm of marine architects, she asked if she could travel with me as Plymouth was on her itinerary. That's all there was to it, my love. When I saw you so unexpectedly that day, the thought uppermost in my mind was the way I had treated you at the casino. So if I had a guilty look it was because of that.

"Now I am done. I could go on longer—begging and pleading, but there comes an end to the words one can use. There will be no need for words when we meet. I shall see my answer in your face.

My love for always,
Harvey."

Kitty slowly put the pages together, folded them and replaced them in the envelope. Her actions were very deliberate. She wanted to savour this moment, not spoil it by a stray movement or rash thought. What she was experiencing was deeper than happiness. She had telegraphed Maggie the day before, giving the times of her train. She knew Harvey would be at Truro or Falmouth to meet her. She looked out of the window at the green folds of the Berkshire countryside and her reflection in the glass stared back at her. Harvey was right. There would be no need for words.